D0204756

MY NAME IS SEEPEETZA

DATE DUE

DEMCO 38-296

Dr. John Woodenlegs Library
1 College Dr.
P.O. Box 98
Lame Deer, MT 59043

MY NAME IS

Seepeetza

❀

Shirley Sterling

A GROUNDWOOD BOOK

Douglas & McIntyre

Toronto   Vancouver   Buffalo

Copyright © 1992 by Shirley Sterling
Sixth printing 1999

All rights reserved. No part of this book may be reproduced, stored in a retrieval
system or transmitted in any form or by any means, without the prior written
permission of the publisher or, in the case of photocopying or other reprographic
copying, a licence from CANCOPY (Canadian Reprography Collective), Toronto,
Ontario.

Groundwood Books/Douglas & McIntyre
585 Bloor Street West
Toronto, Ontario M6G 1K5

Distributed in the U.S.A. by Publishers Group West
1700 Fourth Street
Berkeley, CA 94710

We acknowledge the financial support of the Canada Council for the Arts, the
Ontario Arts Council and the Government of Canada through the Book
Publishing Industry Development Program for our publishing activities.

Canadian Cataloguing in Publication Data

Sterling, Shirley
My name is Seepeetza

"A Groundwood book".
ISBN 0-88899-290-4 (bound) ISBN 0-88899-165-7 (pbk.)

1. Indians of North America - British Columbia -
Juvenile fiction. I. Title.

PS8587.T471M9 1992   jC813'.54   C92094087-0
PZ7.S74My 1992

Design by Michael Solomon
Printed and bound in Canada

ACKNOWLEDGEMENTS

To Sue Ann who wanted to read all the journal
    entries, and so they were written;
to Seraphine Stewart and Charlotte Ned who helped
    me to remember;
to my wonderful family the (Albert) Sterlings of
    Godey, especially Mum;
to Cookie, Rowdy and Pearl, my "little bears of
    spring" who walked me out of the valley of shad-
    ows (sorry I switched a gender);
to Precious, whose novel "My Life Story" written
    at age nine gave me the style and inspiration for
    Seepeetza;
to my Spirit Friend, Sisu Kri, who said a long time
    ago, "You shall know the truth and the truth shall
    set you free."

Thanks to Vivian Moses and Charlotte Saddleman
who appear in the cover photograph.

DEDICATION

To all those who went to the residential schools, and those who tried to help, may you weep and be made free. May you laugh and find your child again. May you recover the treasure that has been lost, the name that gives your life meaning, the mythology by which you can pick up and rebuild the shattered pieces of the past, your own ancient language speaking of ice ages and hairy mammoths, perhaps a little cabin on a grassy hill at the edge of a forest where a grandmother sang a lullaby and made you gloves, or a proud father carved you a whistle out of willow sticks. In celebration of survival I dedicate to you this book, and this poem:

Coyote Laughs

Sometimes at dusk
When Shadowtime steals souls,
I listen as the nighthawk
Screams and falls.
I search the clouds for moonlight . . .

Then somewhere in the pines
Coyote laughs—
Transforming night,
And welcoming the little star
That follows Moon.

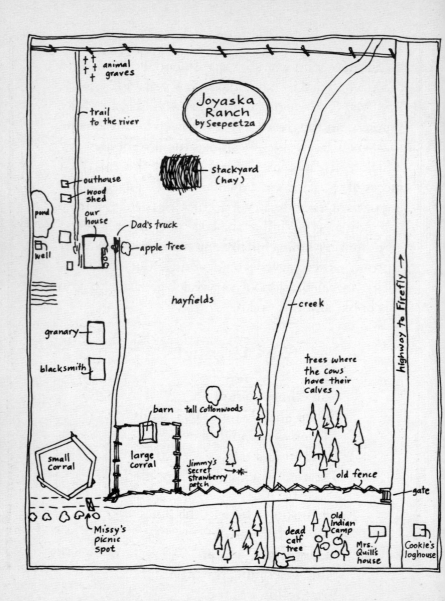

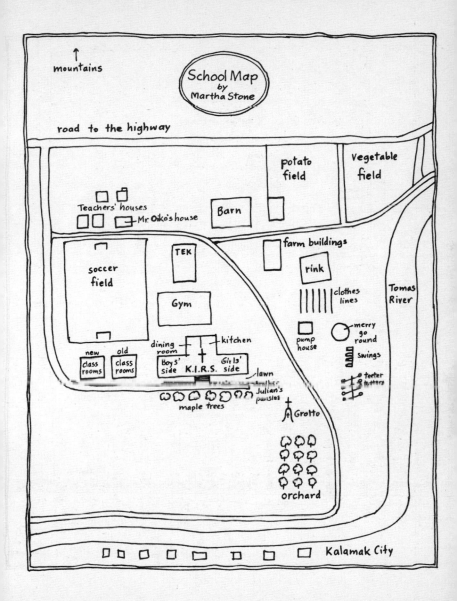

Thursday, September 11, 1958
Kalamak Indian Residential School

TODAY my teacher Mr. Oiko taught us how to write journals. You have to put the date and place at the top of the page. Then you write about what happens during the day. I like journals because I love writing whatever I want. Mr. Oiko says a good way to start is to talk about yourself, where you live, your age, grade, what kind of family you have.

My name is Martha Stone. I am twelve years old in grade six at the Kalamak Indian Residential School. It's next to the Tomas River across from the city of Kalamak, British Columbia.

The school is four storeys high. It's a big red brick building with a church steeple right in the middle above the chapel. The kitchen and dining room are under the chapel. The boys live on the left and the girls live on the right. Next to the river is the school farm where there are dairy cows and vegetable fields.

There are four hundred of us Indian students here and we come from all over B.C. The principal is Father Sloane, a priest. Six other priests here are missionaries. They go to different Indian reserves to say Mass on Sunday. Ten nuns are teachers and girls' supervisors. Sister Theodosia is the intermediate supervisor. We call her Sister Theo.

We are divided into juniors grades one to four, intermediates grades five to eight, and seniors grades nine to twelve. Each group stays in different dormitories called dorms, and recreation rooms called recs. We're not allowed to leave our own rec or dorm except for meals.

The nuns and priests have their own dining rooms, but we eat in the main dining room. There's a wall between the boys' side and girls' side. One of the Sisters watches us eat, but not when we walk back to our recs. That's when my sisters Dorothy and Missy and I sometimes hold hands as we walk down the hall. It's the happiest part of my day.

My best friend is my cousin Cookie. Her mother is Mamie, my mum's sister. Cookie is only my friend sometimes because she's in grade five and mostly she plays with her grade five friends. I told Cookie I want to write secret journals for one year. She won't tell on me. I'll write a short one every day for Mr. Oiko. Then in Thursday library time and on weekends when Sister Theo is busy I'll write this one in a writing tablet titled arithmetic.

I'll get in trouble if I get caught. Sister Theo checks our letters home. We're not allowed to say anything about the school. I might get the strap, or worse. Last year some boys ran away from school because one of the priests was doing something bad to them. The boys were caught and whipped. They had their heads shaved and they had to wear dresses and kneel in the dining room and watch everybody eat. They only had bread and water to eat for a week. Everybody was supposed to laugh at them and make fun of them but nobody did.

I don't like school. We have to come here every September and stay until June. My dad doesn't like it either, but he says it's the law. All status Indian kids have to go to residential schools.

My dad is Frank Stone. He's a rancher. My mum is Marie Stone. I have an older brother called Jimmy. He's eighteen. My sister Dorothy is sixteen. My brother Frank died when he was a baby. He would have been fourteen. My little sister Ann Marie is nine. We call her Missy. My little brother Benjamin is five. We call him Benny. He'll have to come to school here next year when he's six. I have lots of aunts and uncles and cousins at home, and one grandmother. We call her Yay-yah.

We live on Joyaska Ranch near a little town called Firefly. It's about a hundred miles from Kalamak. We get to go home in the summer, at Christmas and sometimes at Easter.

When we're at home we can ride horses, go swimming at the river, run in the hills, climb trees and laugh out loud and holler yahoo anytime we like and we won't get in trouble. At school we get punished for talking, looking at boys in church, even stepping out of line.

I wish I could live at home instead of here.

Thursday, September 18, 1958   K.I.R.S.

TODAY we shucked corn after school. Sister Theo told us to line up on each side of two long tables outside the kitchen. Then Sister Cook sent out some big boxes of corn and we had to pull off the outer skins and corn silk. That's what shucking is, peeling corn. We put the corn and the skins in different boxes. When Sister wasn't looking one of the girls took a bite from the raw corn. Then she passed the corn down the line so we all got a bite. It tasted sweet and juicy. Somebody hid the cobs in the big garbage can filled with corn skins.

Then we all started to get happy, even the big girls. We started joking and laughing like Mum and Aunt Mamie and Yay-yah do when they're cleaning berries or fish together at home. They tell stories and laugh all day while they're working. Sometimes they have to work all night when the fish are running, and still they stay jolly and happy. Dad and Uncle Les bring in lots of fish. Mum cans the fish or dries them on little wooden racks in the sun with a small fire underneath to keep bees off. She puts some sockeye in a crock and salts it.

At home I shuck corn for my mum when she's cooking for my dad's haying crew. There's ten to twenty workers, some with families. They travel by team horses and wagons. We used to too, before Dad got his truck.

One time when my dad was putting up the hay, we had all our wagons and tents in a circle up in the hills above the ranch. Mum cooked for everybody, and we all pitched in and helped. Me and Missy and Benny shucked corn. Dorothy peeled carrots and potatoes. Dad and Jimmy packed water from the creek. Some of the ladies helped Mum cook and tend fire. When the food was ready we ate on tables made of boards. We used logs rolled over as benches. There was lots of talking and laughing, most of it in Indian.

When it got dark some of us kids started playing Hide and Go Seek. That's when I decided to ride the wagon wheel. One family was just moving off to camp a little further down the hill. I grabbed a spoke on their back wagon wheel and hung on as it moved up and around.

"Hold on!" yelled my dad. They stopped the horses, and my dad came running over. That's when I got scared. He told me not to play with the wagon wheels because I might get my head crushed. Mum came over and told all the kids it was time for bed anyway. She made a bed out of fir branches in the back of the wagon for me and Missy and Benny. Then we slept under the stars in warm blankets, listening to Dad and his friends tell stories around the campfire.

You could smell the clay dust in the air, and the fresh cut hay, and the horses and campfire and the wild sage all around us in the hills. Then the coyotes started yapping. Usually we get spooked when we hear them. But this time with everybody camping around us the coyotes sounded friendly. Almost like they were laughing.

Thursday, September 25, 1958 K.I.R.S.

THE first time I really knew about school was when I was five and Cookie came to visit us at home with Aunt Mamie and Uncle Les and her brother Rowdy and her sister Pearl.

"You and me have to go to school next ear," she said.

"What?" I said. Cookie said we had to go to school in Kalamak where Dorothy and Rowdy and Pearl go when they're gone for a long time. We were stunned thinking about going away from home. We couldn't imagine what next ear could be. It sounded awful.

Then one day Dad bought me a suitcase, some new shoes and a wool snowsuit, green like fir trees. Then he drove me to Kalamak. Dorothy went ahead on the cattle truck the school sent to pick up students.

We drove for a long time. Then we came to this big building and Dad parked the truck. Mum walked in with me. The red doors slammed shut behind us and we walked down a long hallway. Our footsteps sounded hollow. When we came to the junior girls rec room we saw a whole bunch of little girls in a big noisy room. Some of them were playing. Some of them were sitting down on red benches with their suitcases, looking sad. A nun called Sister Maura came over and talked to Mum. Then Mum turned and left. I looked at her walking away from me. I heard her footsteps echoing, and I was so scared I felt like I had a giant bee sting over my whole body. Then I stopped feeling anything.

When Mum was gone, Sister grabbed my shoulder and shoved me over to a red bench. She told me not to move. I sat there listening to the girls playing and running back and forth in the rec room. That's when this big girl called Edna came over with her fist raised. "What are you staring at?" she asked.

Just then Sister Maura came back with Cookie. Cookie's eyes looked big and red, like she had been crying. I never saw her look like that before. Sister told her to sit beside me and wait. We were so happy to see each other that we sat on the bench close to each other for a long time.

When Sister Maura came back she made all the girls line up and she put coal oil in our hair to kill nits and lice, even though we didn't have them. She made us get haircuts, take baths and put on smocks, bloomers and undershirts, all exactly alike. We had to put all our own clothes and things in our suitcases which she locked in a storage room. She gave us each a small closet where we put our coats and combs and things. Then she took us upstairs to make our beds. She kept yelling at us to hurry up or Sister Superior would strap us. Sister Superior carries the strap in her sleeve all the time. It looks like a short thick leather belt with a shiny tip. When someone is bad Sister Superior makes them put their hands out, palms up. Then she hits their hands with the strap usually about ten times. When you get used to it it doesn't hurt that much but your hands sting, and you can't help crying.

After that Sister Maura asked me what my name was. I said, my name is Seepeetza. Then she got really mad like I did something terrible. She said never to say that word again. She told me if I had a sister to go and ask what my name was. I went to the intermediate rec and found Dorothy lying on a bench reading comics. I asked her what my name was. She said it was Martha Stone. I said it over and over.

Then I ran back and told Sister Maura. After that she gave me a number, which was 43. She got some of the older girls to teach us how to embroider. Then we had to chain stitch our numbers on all our school clothes.

That night, just before she turned the lights off, Sister Maura taught us how to pray on our knees with our hands folded. Then she told us about devils. She said they were waiting with chains under our beds to drag us into the fires of hell if we got up and left our beds during the night. When she turned the lights off I was scared to move, even to breathe. I knew those devils would come and get me if I made a sound. I kept really still.

Then I heard a small sound like a whistle. I wondered what it was. It reminded me of Spud our dog, the time he got porcupine quills in his nose. My dad told him to lie down and be quiet. Then my dad pulled out the quills with a pair of pliers. Spud kept making that whistling noise over and over as my dad pulled out the quills.

Someone was crying. I wanted to cry too, but I didn't dare make any noise. A long time later I was still too afraid to get up to use the bathroom. In the morning my bed was wet and Sister Superior strapped me. I had to wear a sign to the dining room saying, I am a dirty wetbed.

EDNA asked for a fight again this afternoon. She came up to me when Sister was out of the rec and twisted my arm around my back before I knew she was behind me. She shoved me into a book case so it looked like we were just talking.

"You think you're so smart," she said. "Don't you?" I didn't say anything. I was trying to keep my eyes from getting tears. She was hurting me, and I was really scared. She's a lot bigger than me. She's in grade six too, but she's fourteen. She failed two grades.

"I think you're chicken," she said. When someone says that it means they want to fight. I didn't move.

"You blue eyes," she sneered. "You dirty sha-mah. How does it feel to look like a white?"Sometimes I look out the dorm window at the Tomas River and I wish I could hide under the water and never come out. I look at the stars at night and wish I could travel a million miles into outer space and never come back.

I would like to punch Edna in the stomach even if she beat me up. But I couldn't stand it if the girls took her side and crowded around me and called me that awful name.

A couple of grade eight girls from her hometown

came running over asking what the matter was. Edna let me go and whispered something in their ears. They looked at me and ran away laughing, making noises like a chicken.

I stood there staring at the wall for a minute, rubbing my arm. It was red where she twisted it. Then I went into the lavatory to wash my face. I'm not allowed to drink anything after five o'clock. Sometimes even the water in the toilet tank looks tempting.

When we were junior girls we used to have gangs. There was one from Williams Lake, Prince George, Kamloops, even one from Firefly. The girls in a gang stuck up for each other. They got mad at girls from other towns. They said, what are you staring at, or liar liar pants on fire. The gang from Chase was the toughest. Sometimes when Sister was out of the rec they used to fight with other gangs. They used to roll on the floor with everybody cheering. When the lookout girl said, "Sister's coming," everybody would jump up and pretend nothing happened, because the worst thing you can be in this school is a snitch. You don't ever tell on anyone here.

MY favourite place here is the library. It's small and dark, with four shelves. It's in the basement of the new classroom building. We get library there on Thursday afternoons before supper.

When I come here I feel so happy. I look at the books and my heart beats faster. When I read a book it's like going away to a different place. Like living a different life, much more exciting than mine. We're allowed to take out two books at a time for one week. Last year I was not allowed to take books out for one whole month because I was reading too much in class.

I like the horse books like *The Black Stallion*, and the Beau Geste books about the French Foreign Legion, and the Freckles books about loggers. I like Trixie Belden and Nancy Drew books too, but the Tarzan books are the best.

I took out *Moby Dick* once but it was hard to read. It took me a long time because the words are big and the print is small. Mr. Oiko raised his eyebrows when he saw me reading it. He asked me why don't I read *Anne of Green Gables*. I tried it but it's not interesting. Anne's biggest problem was that Gilbert called her carrots.

Mr. Oiko talks funny, because he's from Prince Edward Island. When he says "was" he says it like "wuss" instead of "wuz." He's nice but I don't think he knows much about teaching. He writes things on the board which he doesn't explain very well, like prepositions and adverb phrases. And sometimes he gets mad.

Once when he left the room for a minute everybody started throwing spitballs and talking. It was the only time we ever did this. When he came back he yelled at us and said we all have to stay after school till four o'clock. We were scared because we'd really get in trouble with Sister Theo if she found out. Without thinking I said, "You stinker." Dorothy says that all the time and people think it's cute. But Mr. Oiko sent me right out of class to the rec to tell Sister Theo. I was scared she'd clobber me on the back like usual, but all she did was make me darn socks all day.

Another time Mr. Oiko strapped two boys for fooling around at the back of the class. He made them bend over in front of everyone. One of them passed gas while he strapped them. After that I behaved myself.

Mr. Oiko asked me to babysit his baby once. He got permission from Sister Theo, so I walked over to his house on the other side of the soccer field. His wife is named Michelle. She's French Canadian. She's really pretty. I don't know why she married Mr. Oiko. He's not very handsome. He has a round red face and curly yellow hair. Michelle can't speak English, so Mr. Oiko told me what to do. The baby went right to sleep in its crib, so I just sat there and read a book. They were gone for about one hour. They paid me fifty cents.

Thursday, October 16, 1958 *K.I.R.S.*

AT school we get up at six o'clock every morning. As soon as Sister rings the bell, we kneel on the floor and say our prayers. Then we get up and take turns washing and brushing our teeth. We're not allowed to talk. When we are dressed in our uniforms, Sister marches us in lines two by two to chapel for Mass. We go down on one knee before we slide into the pews to kneel down. We sneak looks at the boys on the other side of the chapel.

After Mass we put our smocks over our uniforms and line up for breakfast in the hall outside the dining room. We can talk then because Sister goes for breakfast in the Sisters' dining room. They get bacon or ham, eggs, toast and juice. We can see when they open the door and go in for breakfast. We get gooey mush with powder milk and brown sugar. We say grace before and after every meal.

After breakfast we have jobs to do like clean the lavatories or dust the halls and sweep stairs. After jobs are finished we put our smocks in our closets and line up in the rec room to go to class.

My class, grade six, is in the old classroom building. Mr. Oiko teaches catechism, composition, spelling and arithmetic in the morning, and science, socials and art in the afternoon. At noon we come back to the rec room to put our smocks on again to have lunch. Lunch is usually soup.

After school we change into our own clothes, usually jeans and blouses. Then Sister sends us outside, even if it's cold, and everybody gets an apple. If we're dancers we go and practise or decorate our costumes with sequins.

Dancers give up every second weekend to go places and perform. People clap for a long time and we get top marks at the B.C. Interior Music Festival.

We hardly ever make a mistake when we are performing. It's not just because we know we'll get punished, but also because we practise every day after school when everybody else is listening to the radio and reading magazines and going for walks outside.

Once somebody asked me right on stage who was my teacher. I got mixed up and said Mr. Oiko was. Sister almost had a fit right there behind the curtain. "I'm your dance teacher, you amathon," she hissed at me after.

Supper is usually cabbage stew, two slices of bread with margarine, and wrinkled apples for dessert. Friday night is my favourite because we get oatmeal cookies for dessert. Once I found a worm in my soup. When I told Sister Theo she told me not to be ungrateful. There were starving children in Africa.

We don't get margarine at every meal so some of the girls stick some to the bottom of the table. Then at the next meal they scrape it off and spread it on their bread. Other times girls hide bread or raw carrots in their bloomer legs under the elastic. They take it out and eat it late at night when the lights are out. That's when we get really hungry. We heard that the boys tie a jack knife to a string and lower it through a small window into the cellar. They spear potatoes and carrots that way, and eat them.

We play in the rec after supper, except for the dancers who practise instead. At eight o'clock we go upstairs to the dorm, wash up and say prayers. Then Sister puts out the light.

Saturday is our big work day. We scrub all the floors all in a line on our knees. We wax the floors, wait for the wax to dry, then shine them by pulling each other around the floor on old wool blankets. We scrub toilets and stairs, shine windows and dust furniture and window sills. We always get beans for supper on Saturday.

On Sunday morning we go to High Mass. The girls have to wear navy blue tams. At home the women wear kerchiefs. Father Sloane wears gold and white vestments. I like Sunday mornings because we get cornflakes for breakfast.

THIS morning I got a parcel from home. I was so happy when Sister Theo came into the recreation room and called my name. My white name, that is. Not Seepeetza anymore, or Tootie, or McSpoot which only my dad calls me.

"Martha Stone, you have a parcel," she said. Sister handed the brown package to me and said I could take only one thing from my parcel every day at recess. The rest she would keep in the closet with the other parcels.

"Yes, Sister," I said. That's all we're allowed to say to the Sisters, yes Sister or no Sister.

I took my parcel over to a bench to open it. A bunch of girls followed me to see what I got.

"Who's it from? Who's it from?" they asked.

I looked at the name in the corner. J. Stone. My brother Jimmy. I smiled. Jimmy must have wrapped the parcel in the kitchen with my mum helping. Imagine. Just a few days ago this parcel was at home. My mum must have touched it! Maybe she put something in it and said, "Seepeetza will need this."

I pulled off the brown paper. Opened the little skinny box. The intermediate girls crowded in closer.

"Oh," we all said together.

There was a bag of marshmallows, a package of cookies with coconut over marshmallow, fancy ones. My mum and dad never buy these kind. They cost too much. There was a bag of toffees in shiny wrap and colourful wax paper, some peanuts and peppermints. A treasure.

"Take one thing and bring the rest back, miss," yelled Sister. Her face was red.

I tore open the marshmallow bag. I took two. I sneaked one to the biggest of the girls around me.

"Share," I whispered. I put the other marshmallow in my pocket. Every once in a while I take a tiny bite and keep it in my mouth for a long time. That way I'll still have a piece in my hand when I go to sleep tonight. I'll fall asleep thinking of home.

Thursday, October 30, 1958 K.I.R.S.

MY brother Jimmy doesn't go to school in Kalamak anymore. He goes to the white school in Firefly. Maybe the school people don't know he's Indian. He has dark red hair and green eyes.

At home, my mum and dad get up at four o'clock in the morning to get him ready for school. It's still dark at four. My dad gets up first to light the coal oil lamp and make fires in the cookstove and in the big heater in the living room. When the fires are crackling my mum gets up and cooks breakfast. Her mush is nice. It's not gooey. We have it with real cream from the cow, and homemade bread and butter. My mum makes a nice lunch for Jimmy, a Thermos of hot tea, homemade bread and butter with sharp cheese, a piece of apple pie and an apple. He has to walk two miles.

One morning Jimmy wouldn't get up when my dad called him, so my dad poured a bucket of ice-cold water on him. He told Jimmy to go to school and get an education. Jimmy never tried to sleep in again.

Dorothy got in trouble in school because of her red hair once. Some girls climbed over the fence and took apples from the orchard because they were hungry. Old Brother Julian came along and caught them. The only one he recognized was Dorothy because of her hair, so she got the strap. Some girls think she's a white, and they call her shamah. They say it like a dirty word. They ask me sometimes if I'm a shamah because I have green eyes. That's one reason I don't have many friends here.

My brother Jimmy hates Kalamak Indian Residential School. He calls it KIRS, or "curse." He went there in the junior grades. One day my dad went to Kalamak to interpret in court. After he finished his court business he went to see Jimmy but the priests wouldn't let him. They said Jimmy was busy working in the vegetable fields. My dad got mad and took Jimmy out and sent him to the town school in Firefly where he joined the cadets, baseball, basketball and the track team. I wish my dad would take me out of Kalamak Indian School too, but we'd get in trouble with the law.

Every night when we're at home Jimmy plays his guitar and sings songs, usually country and western or Elvis songs like Blue Suede Shoes.

Dorothy doesn't mind Kalamak School but the rest of us hate it. She likes classes. Her marks are in the nineties. I think she got tired of babysitting Benny and Missy and me when we were little. Maybe that's why she likes school.

One time Missy asked Mum if she could quit school. I got jealous because I thought they were going to let her. Mum said her grandmother, Quaslametko, didn't want her and her brothers and sisters to go to school, because school would turn them into white people. They wouldn't be able to hunt or fish or make baskets or anything useful anymore.

Saturday, November 1, 1958 *K.I.R.S.*

HALLOWEEN was last night. After supper we all got bags with peanuts in them and two Halloween candies with orange and black wax paper, and red apples and best of all, an oatmeal cookie. A big one.

Some of the girls saved their treats so they could eat them today. Cookie and I ate ours right away.

Cookie said we'd better eat our treats or else one of the bigger girls might take them away from us.

After supper we got to wear our Halloween hats and dance to music in the gym. All the intermediate and high school students went, boys and girls. Mostly we jive or waltz at school dances. Sometimes we do the broom dance. We pass around the broom until the music stops. Then whoever was holding it last gets spanked with it. Lots of girls dance with each other. It takes a few dances before the boys get brave enough to walk across the floor to the girls' side to ask for a dance. Charlie usually asks me to dance but he didn't come back to school this year. Maybe he went to Coqualeetza. That's where kids go if they get T B, tuberculosis. He's kind of skinny, Charlie.

We made our orange and black paper hats in the rec after school last week. Sister gave us paper, glue and scissors. Mostly everybody made witch hats with a tall point and a brim and some thin strips of paper hanging off the top. Me too. Sister told us there was a prize for the best hat. The prize was free candy from the store. The store is just a little closet where Sister keeps candy for sale and the parcels we get from home. I tried hard to win, but I didn't.

It's funny. We all thought we had the best one, but Adelia won. She's the only one who is allowed to keep her long hair because it's naturally curly.

Sister Theo says long straight hair makes us look like wild Indians. The rest of us have our hair cut short with bangs, and straight around like a bowl.

Adelia used to be the queen of the junior girls. During free time a lot of girls would crowd around her and ask her to tell them stories. They put their kerchiefs on her shoulders like a cape. They gave her candies and gum and comics. She was kind of bossy, always telling the girls what games to play outside, and who to pick on. I didn't pay any attention to them because I was always reading. Besides, I didn't want to kiss her hand like some of them did.

Then one day when I was reading, some of Adelia's friends came and stood around me and asked why I was so jealous of Adelia. Sure enough, Edna was one of them. She had her cheeks blown into a big pout, and her hands on her hips. I was pretty scared until Cookie's big sister Pearl came over and asked what was going on. Those girls said nothing, and they ran away.

When we became intermediates we stopped having queens because Sister Theo is always around keeping an eye on us.

Thursday, November 6, 1958 K.I.R.S.

I GET excited when it's November because we get to go home for Christmas on December 21st. I can't breathe when I think about it. I wish it was right now.

Another thing too. Mum sends our winter coats and boots in the middle of November. I can't wait. My feet get cold when I walk to class, even though it's not that far. My legs ache at night because our sheets are cold. Some girls sleep together to keep warm, but Sister gets mad and makes them go back to their own beds. Once one of the girls pushed her blankets off in her sleep. Sister saw her and came over to tuck her in. I wished she would come and tuck me in too. Next night some of the other girls tried it but Sister just got mad at them.

At home Mum makes all our clothes, even coats. She takes apart big clothes and makes all kinds of things from them. In the summer she makes us pedal pushers and dresses out of cotton flour sacks. Once she made me a blue satin bathing suit. Sometimes Missy and I fall asleep under the sewing machine when Mum sews late at night. We play under the table with pieces of cloth until we get tired and fall asleep. Mum wakes us up and tells us it's time to go to bed. She picks up the coal oil lamp and takes us into our room. Then she tucks us in. At first the sheets are cold. Then it warms up and stays warm all night. Missy and I rub toes. When it's really cold Mum heats up an iron on the stove and wraps it up in a towel to put at our feet. It's nice and warm.

Sometimes when my dad doesn't come home till

late we climb into bed with my mum. She's so warm. She smells nice. She lets us put our cold feet on her legs. When my dad comes home he tells us to get into our own bed. One time when I was really small I got to sleep in between my mum and my dad. My dad's longjohns felt warm. I never get scared of the dark when my dad is home.

We have green wool blankets and homemade quilts at home. Mum made the quilts. They're all colours. They are thick and heavy. She calls them her patchworks. The blankets at school are grey.

We have two stoves at home, a cookstove in the kitchen and a wood heater in the living room. The heater is like a big rectangle box. You can put large pieces of wood in it and it burns all night. Our cookstove takes small pieces of wood. It has an oven and round burners. There's a water reservoir on the side that we fill up every day for washing dishes, and two heavy irons Mum heats up for ironing clothes. Every day Jimmy chops wood. He packs in big pieces for the heater. When we're home me and Missy pack in small pieces. Benny packs in the kindling.

It smells real nice in the kitchen when there's fresh chopped wood and wood smoke. I like it when the kettle whistles. It sounds like music, and the kettle rattles back and forth on the stove with a beat. Ta, ta, tum. Ta, ta, tum.

SISTER Theo got mad at me for daydreaming again. I was standing at the dorm window staring at the fresh snow on the fields along the river this morning. I should have been mopping the dust under the beds.

I was shocked when Sister yelled my name. She usually doesn't come up to the dorm after breakfast. She grabbed the back of my tunic and pushed me all the way across the dorm, down the hall and into the broom closet and shoved me at the mops. She said, "Don't let me catch you daydreaming again, you lazy amathon."

I can't help it. I can't stop thinking of home. I keep remembering what it's like to go riding horses all summer and help my dad put up the hay.

We start early in the morning before the sun is up because it gets too hot to work in the afternoon. We take pitchforks and load the hay onto the sloop. Then my dad drives the horses to the stackyard, hooks them up to the trip rope, and the horses pull the hay in a sling up to the top of the two poles over the stack. The load swings back and forth. When it's right over the top of the stack my dad hollers, "Trip," and I pull the trip rope and the sling comes apart and the hay falls on top of the stack.

The best part is riding on top of the hay sloop back to the stack. We all sit in a row facing the back and tease each other. Sometimes my dad lets me drive the horses. He showed me how to swing wide at the stackyard gate so we don't bump the gatepost. When I drive the horses I think this is what I want to do when I grow up. Live on a ranch with horses. Dad says I have to be a nurse or a teacher but I would like to be an interpreter like him. He speaks lots of Indian languages, but he won't teach us. Mum won't either. She says the nuns and priests will strap us. I wonder why it's bad.

We get stomach aches when we have to come back to school after summer. It starts when we see the first leaves turning yellow at the end of August. It's usually the tall cottonwoods near Cody Creek or some of the river trees at Big Rock. One minute we are laughing and playing. The next minute we are afraid. Missy asks, do you think the leaves are turning yellow now? I say yes. We look at each other with sick eyes. Then we walk home so we can be near Mum.

When I hear the red doors slam behind me at school it's like I get a numb feeling over my whole body and I'm hiding way down inside myself. I don't really hear or see what's going on around me. Just sort of. It's like a buzzing that's far away. I wake up when Sister calls my name. By then she's mad and I'm in trouble, and I feel awful.

Last year Father Sloane took some pictures of us when we were in our dancing costumes at the Irish Concert. It was funny because I was smiling in those pictures. I looked happy. How can I look happy when I'm scared all the time?

Thursday, November 20, 1958 K.I.R.S.

I BURIED the doll today. Somebody from town gave the school some old dolls, and Sister gave one to me. It had a hard face and messy brown hair. Its eyes could open and close. It had eyelashes. Sister looked mad when she gave the dolls out, like it was a nuisance. Then she told us to go outside and play. The wind was blowing and I was so cold my hands felt numb. I went on the other side of the teeter-totters where there is soft sand, and I dug a hole and put the doll in it and covered it up so it would be safe from the cold.

My mum made me a doll once, a rag doll. She made it out of scraps on her sewing machine. It had yellow flowers on it. Then Missy wanted it so Mum gave it to her and made me another one. It had black and white stripes and I didn't like it. Anyway I'm too busy for dolls at home. I have to help my dad with the horses and everything.

After I buried the doll I looked up and saw this grade eight girl called Maryann watching me. She said she was a grandmother, and she had stsa-wen. I was surprised to hear her say that word. It means dried fish. I thought only we knew that word from home. She handed me an old dried piece of pine wood and told me to sit on the ground to eat my stsa-wen. We sat cross-legged on the ground facing each other near an old log so we could keep warm. The tumbleweeds were rolling past and the wind was kind of moaning.

Sometimes when it's this cold we make tumbleweed houses or find a big cardboard box at the incinerator, climb inside and close the flaps. It's nice because we can keep warm and tell stories. When it's warmer out we play Auntie Auntie I Over with a rubber ball at the pump house. It's a little red hut with water pipes in it and a water pump. We throw the ball over it and run around to try and catch it on the other side. There are swings and a merry-go-round and teeter-totters in the playground, but I don't like them. They make me dizzy.

It's my cousin Mickey's fault I get dizzy because he gave me some chewing tobacco once when we were waiting in the truck outside the beer parlour for my dad. My dad came whistling around the corner and started up the truck at the same time I put some in my mouth. The smell of the gas and the taste of the snoose made me sick to my stomach. I fell down at the back of the truck and spat it out but the taste stayed for a long time. To this day I get car sick. I get sick on swings. I get sick tumbling in gym class.

Maryann surprised me by talking Indian. We're

not supposed to. She ordered me to eat all my fish
just like she was a real grandmother. We laughed. "I
wish it was really fish," she said. "And I wish I was
home with grandmother. My parents are dead." She
asked me if we ate dried salmon too. I nodded. Then
she whispered, "Sister's coming." We threw away
the wood and jumped up and started running in
because Sister was ringing the bell for supper.

Thursday, December 4, 1958 *K.I.R.S.*

I CAME back from the hospital today. I had an
abscessed tooth. Two weeks ago I woke up with a
lump on my cheek. When the lump grew to the size
of a marble and got blue, Sister Theo sent me to see
Sister Nurse. The next thing I knew Brother Pitt was
driving me to the hospital in the blue Volkswagen
bus. Brother Pitt squints and talks in a gruff voice.
He has a red nose. "Get in," he growled, flinging
the car door open. When I got in he slammed it shut
with a loud bang.

The hospital where I went is made of red bricks,
like school. My nurse was Miss Murdoch. I was at
the children's ward in a room with a window, a
bathroom and two beds. In the next room there was
a boy who had been burned in a house fire. Most of
the time he had medicine to make him sleep, but
sometimes he woke up at night and cried. Miss Mur-

doch wouldn't let me visit him. She said I might give him germs and make him die. She made me stay in my room.

I liked it in the hospital. Father Sloane came to visit me and he let me wear his relic around my neck. It's a tiny piece of bone from one of the saints that he keeps in a round gold case like a watch. Father Sloane said sometimes miracles happen because of the saints. He brought me lots of comics that he collected from the junior boys. Miss Murdoch came in three times a day with my pills. I swallowed them with a tiny paper cupful of water. She asked how I was doing and talked to me for awhile.

There was another girl in my room. Her name was Miyoki, a Japanese girl. She was fourteen. Her parents came to see her every day. They brought her treats like pop and chips and comics. Sometimes they gave me chips too. They talked to me a few times but mostly they just smiled and said hello. After Miyoki's parents left we read our comics and traded. Miyoki and I both love art. I draw horses and she draws fruit or flowers. Mum and Dad would have come right over if they knew I was in the hospital. I guess Father Sloane never told them.

I wasn't scared to sleep there but I still wouldn't let my hands or feet dangle over the edge of the bed. I thought the devils might have followed me to the hospital. Mostly I just thought about home before I went to sleep.

My dad likes Japanese people. He guarded them in a camp near Firefly during World War II, and he learned some Japanese words from them. They told him about medicine tea. Sometimes he hunted deer for them. Once my brother Jimmy called them Japs and my dad took him in the woodshed and whipped him. Both my dad and Jimmy cried.

When my lump went away Miss Murdoch told me it was time to go back to school. She thought I would be happy, but I wasn't. She gave me my tunic, my blouse and blazer and told me to get dressed. My brown oxfords felt heavy. That's when I knew I had gotten weak from lying in bed too much. When Brother Pitt came with the bus to pick me up I told him my shoes felt heavy. He didn't seem to hear me. "Get in," he growled.

Thursday, December 11, 1958 K.I.R.S.

I NEVER thought Sister Theo was our friend before. She's always yelling orders and bawling us out, but Dorothy said Sister helped her out of a scrape.

Dorothy goes to classes at St. Mark's now, the Catholic high school in town. All the students in grade ten, eleven and twelve do. Brother Pitt drives them in a yellow school bus every day.

Anyway, Dorothy had some exams to write and her supervisor wouldn't let her study for them. The senior girls have a really mean Sister. Her name is Sister Kerr. She walks like a man, tough looking, and she talks in a gruff voice. She uses judo on the girls to make them obey. Sometimes when they are scrubbing the floor on their knees she kicks them on the behind to make them go faster.

She really hates Dorothy. "You Stones think you're so smart," she sneers. "But I'm going to take you down a peg or two." She makes Dorothy clean toilets and work in the kitchen washing dishes.

Sister Kerr sends the senior girls to bed at eight o'clock every night even though they have a lot of homework to do. At first Dorothy took her books to the little lavatory in the hall outside their dorm and studied there for awhile. But then the watchman reported to Sister Kerr that someone had that light on very late at night. Sister Kerr started patrolling the halls after that and Dorothy didn't know what to do. That's when she told Sister Theo about it. Sister Theo found Dorothy a flashlight so she could study under her blankets at night. After that Sister Theo fixed up a study place for Dorothy behind the piano in the intermediate rec. They put a blanket over it so the watchman wouldn't see the light. Sister Theo told Dorothy not to tell Sister Kerr about it because the supervisors are not supposed to interfere with each other.

Dorothy told me some of the teachers are mad at Sister Theo because she's in charge of the dancers.

They don't like the dancers getting special things like trips out of town and extra clothes. They say we don't get our homework done. Sometimes I wish we could quit dancing and concerts. I love basketball and track and field. I'm the second fastest sprinter in school. I can do the hundred yard dash in thirteen seconds. But dancers are not allowed to join track meets because we might get hurt. We wouldn't be able to perform. Also Father Sloane says we have to give other girls a chance to take part in things.

Anyway, I don't know why Sister Kerr thinks us Stones think we're smart. I just hope she's gone by the time I get to high school.

Thursday, December 18, 1958 K.I.R.S.

MR. Oiko made us grade six girls sing Wake Up Little Suzy at the Christmas concert last night. We didn't really sing. Mr. Oiko played a record and we just pretended to sing. He told us to wear tight skirts and pullover sweaters. On stage we had to line up in a half circle and snap our fingers like Elvis and dance in place to the music. Half the girls couldn't keep time, and we were all scared to look jazzy. The song seemed to go on and on and on. I could feel the sweat on my face and I didn't know where to look. I never felt so stupid in my whole life.

Only grades one to eight were in the concert.

Most of the classes sang carols or recited something. The grade threes had a rhythm band. They hit triangles and cymbals to every second beat of a song on a record. Everybody likes the Christmas concert because we get to practise during class time, so we don't have to do lessons.

I'm so happy because tomorrow is the last day of school. Father Jeremy, the missionary for Firefly, will be driving me and Missy and Dorothy home right after supper tomorrow so we can sing some carols at one of the churches. We get to go home a day early. Everybody else is going home on Saturday. Sister is going to let me pack my suitcase today after school.

We made Christmas cards for our parents in art class. I made Mum one with jingle bells on it because she remembers them from when she was a little girl. She says, "Ahhh," with a big smile on her face when she hears bells. I made Dad a card with a picture of a fir tree in the woods with snow on the branches. It reminds me of the times we go to get wood in the winter. My dad hitches up the horses to the hay sloop and we all bundle up in warm clothes and go out into the hills. Dad and Jimmy cut down dead trees and cut them into blocks. The rest of us chop off branches or load the blocks onto the sloop. Then we ride home in the snow and unload the blocks at the woodshed, and Mum makes us cocoa.

The first thing I want to do when I get home is

take Spud for a walk up the hill and look for a good Christmas tree. Then I'll show Jimmy. Jimmy is the one who got our first Christmas tree. He chopped down a little fir tree. He put the tree on a crate by the window in our living room. He put popcorn on a string and wrapped it around the tree. Then Mum made some red ribbon bows for it and Dorothy made paper birds that she learned how to do in school. When my dad saw the tree he took me and Missy to town and bought some shiny glass balls with all different colours on them. Missy picked out the star. It's all shiny like a looking-glass.

Thursday, December 25, 1958   Joyaska Ranch

COOKIE, Rowdy and Pearl invited me to stay overnight at their log house last night. I asked Mum if I could because I wanted to see if we heard any ghost footsteps walking around the stove. They told me they sometimes heard footsteps but when they lit the lamp or turned on the flashlight there was no one there. I didn't tell my mum that. She wouldn't have let me go.

She said I could, and I walked over in the snow to their place after supper. It's about half a mile. First we read all their comics. Then after Aunt Mamie and Uncle Les went out to visit friends we read Aunt Mamie's True Confessions for awhile. One story was called, "I stole my daughter's boyfriend." It was about this divorced mother who got mixed up with her daughter's boyfriend.

We put the True Confessions back exactly where we found them because we are not allowed to read them. Then we cracked nuts and played Snap with Rowdy. He asked me if Jimmy was going to go drinking again. I was surprised. I said I didn't know Jimmy drank. Rowdy wouldn't say any more about it. After that we watched Pearl put on nail polish as she talked about this guy she likes called Arnie Sam. I said I was glad Charlie didn't come back to school so I don't have to get a stupid valentine card from him this year. After that we got sleepy. I climbed into bed with Cookie and Pearl. We told spooky stories. Then I fell asleep.

I dreamed about three bears. I was up at the gate looking through to the other side when I heard their voices deep and whispery. I was so frightened I could hardly take in what they were saying. They were about ten feet away looking at me. Two spoke to me and the third came up and touched me and turned me white like I had frost all over me. I woke up with a start, freezing cold.

I looked around. It was almost daylight and I could see Cookie's parents sleeping in bed at the far end of the bedroom. Cookie and Pearl were still sound asleep, one on each side of me. I covered myself up and went back to sleep.

———

After breakfast I walked home and found Mum in the kitchen. It smelled like spices and apples and fresh-baked bread and ham and turkey baking in the oven. Mum handed me a brown shopping bag, my Christmas treat. We all get one every year. It was half-filled with oranges, hard candies, ribbon candies, toffee, gumdrops, bubblegum, Crackerjack popcorn, nuts and special red apples Dad orders from Sears.

I went into the living room to look at our Christmas tree all sparkling with tinsel, icicles and coloured glass balls. Jimmy and Dorothy decorated it. I dug into my bag and ate all the soft gumdrops first, then the toffees. After I ate two oranges Mum told me to save my appetite for turkey dinner. I told her about my bear dream. She stopped peeling carrots and looked at me for a long time. Then she told me all about becoming a woman. It sounds like the most godawful thing that ever was.

Thursday, December 31, 1958   Indian Meadows

MUM'S mad. This morning my dad and a bunch of his pals came home with some Scotch whisky to celebrate the New Year. So Mum and Jimmy harnessed the horses to the sleigh and took us up to Indian Meadows. It's six miles up into the mountains where Uncle Tommy and his family live on a little ranch. Yay-yah lives next door. Uncle Tommy is Mum's brother.

It was about noon when we left Joyaska Ranch. Mum bundled us all up nice and warm in two pants and sweaters each and warm winter coats. We put on thick wool socks and gumboots, hats and scarves. Then Mum told Jimmy to put dry hay on the sleigh and she put blankets over it. The hay smelled sweet. Mum told us to sit close to each other, and she put wool blankets over us. Mum and Jimmy sat in the front seat taking turns to drive the horses.

The sun was sparkling on the snow. We saw little snow birds flitting among the fir trees and all kinds of tracks in the snow, rabbit tracks, bird tracks and even deer tracks. We passed people on the road and they waved at us, smiling because we were riding a sleigh. Most people were driving cars. As the horses trotted along we sang Jingle Bells, Frosty the Snow-man, Rudolph the Red-Nosed Reindeer, then some Christmas carols. We didn't feel cold, but our noses were all red.

It was just getting dark when we got to Uncle's log house. My cousin Sonny was packing water when he must have heard the harness jingling. He looked at us smiling for a minute. Then he went inside to call Uncle. He told his dad, "Looks like Mrs. Santa and a whole bunch of Rudolphs just pulled in from the North Pole." My uncle and aunt and Yay-yah came out smiling and looked at us for a moment.

"Where's Frank?" they asked Mum.

"Drinking at the house," said Mum.

Uncle's eyebrows went up. "Ohhh," he said.

"Well, come in," said Aunt Ella. "I'll make you some tea and thaw you out." Tea was grouse soup, deer roast, dried salmon, mashed potatoes, mashed turnips, macaroni, rice, gravy, hot biscuits with butter, fruitcake, canned peaches and huckleberry jam.

While Mum and Auntie and Yay-yah were cooking, Uncle and Jimmy went out to put the horses in the barn and feed them the hay that Mum brought. Now Mum and Aunt Ella are doing the dishes, and Dorothy is sitting on Uncle's bed telling stories to the little kids, Benny and Missy, Annie and Mary May. Uncle, Jimmy and Sonny are packing in wood. Every time they open the door a cloud of steam leaves the house. That means it's really cold outside. Uncle told us we might as well spend the night, so we are.

Me and Yay-yah are sitting at the table near the coal oil lamp. The radio is playing an Elvis song, Are You Lonesome Tonight. Yay-yah is mending a pair of beaded gloves. She looked at me over her spectacles for awhile and watched me writing. I told her I'm writing a story. She chuckled and went back to her sewing.

I like Uncle's house. It's one big room with a loft upstairs for Sonny. It has a black and white cookstove, a big heavy table made out of planks, heavy benches and two double beds at the far end of the room. There's thick wooden pegs for coats hammered into the logs beside the door, and a plank above it for putting hats. Mostly all the men around here wear cowboy hats, except when it's freezing cold. Uncle's war medals, guitar, rifle and scabbard are hanging on the wall above his bed.

Uncle Tommy is a deer hunter and a sharpshooter like my dad. Sometimes to practise target shooting they hammer a nail partways into a log. Then they stand from a hundred yards away and drive the nail in by shooting it.

Uncle told my mum we could stay as long as we like. I think we'll stay a couple of days and then go home, when Dad's finished partying. When we get home he'll have the house nice and clean and he'll buy a big bunch of groceries.

In the meantime we're going sledding tomorrow at the little hill at the end of the hay field. Sonny and Jimmy and Uncle are going riding, which means they might hunt. The ladies will visit and cook and tell stories.

I hope Uncle plays his guitar after. He sings western songs, him and Aunt Ella together. She has a high voice. I like the way they sing Forever My Darling. Later when it's midnight, Uncle and Sonny and Jimmy will go out and shoot in the New Year. Then we'll all sing Old Lang Syne and it will be 1959. Imagine, 1959! I hope I can stay awake for it.

SISTER Theo looks just like the wicked witch in the Wizard of Oz. She wears a black dress down to her shoes. Her shoes are black too. She doesn't have a witch hat but a black veil with a white thing around the edge. You can't see her hair. She has a big nose and small shiny eyes and thin lips. When she gets mad her right shoulder lifts, and her head twitches to the side. She has a cross around her neck, and big brown rosary beads hanging down her side. You can hear them clicking when she walks down the hallway. We know she's coming, and we run. All the Sisters dress like that.

Yesterday Sister really scared a little boy. His mum was bringing his older sister back to school from the holidays. Sister Theo saw them and walked up to welcome them. She's nice to parents. That little boy saw Sister coming and he started to back away from her. His eyes were big and his mouth was open. "Are you a witch?" he squeaked. Poor Sister looked hurt. I guess that little boy never saw a nun before. We all looked away. My mum tells us never to stare at people.

My mum is pretty. She has long black hair and big brown eyes like Dorothy. When my mum brushes her hair it spreads out in little waves all down her back. I like watching her brush her hair. Sometimes she stops brushing and lets me run my fingers through her hair. Then she braids it and winds it like a little crown around her head. It's neat and tidy that way, she says. When she goes to town she wears a little hat that curves down to one side.

When my mum speaks she speaks softly. She smiles and laughs a lot. There's this little song she sings when she is washing the dishes or sewing, or holding a baby. It has no words and it sounds happy and sad at the same time. When she sings that song nobody talks. It makes me think of a wonderful faraway land where the grass is so green it's like the crayon pictures we used to draw in grade one. It's happy there, and when you come back you want to be the kindest person who ever lived. I asked Mum what she was singing once, and she said, "Oh, just a little song."

Mum likes it when it rains or snows. When it rains she looks out the window and says her tiger lilies will grow. When it snows she says it reminds her of Christmas when she was a little girl and her dad was the blacksmith. He told her and her brothers and sisters that if they were really good, Santa would bring them something. They had to wash their cotton stockings and hang them up beside the heater stove. On Christmas morning they would run to the stockings to see if they got anything. Sure enough, they got candies and apples. Sometimes there were oranges, but they were really small and dried out.

My mum said she didn't mind, because it was a treat to get them at all.

She said in those days in the winter they went everywhere with horses and sleighs, and there were real jingle bells on the harnesses. She was born in 1915, when nobody had cars in Firefly.

Thursday, January 15, 1959 *K.I.R.S.*

MY birthday was two days ago. Now I'm thirteen, a teenager. But I don't feel any different. Sister Theo made everybody stand in a circle in the rec and sing Happy Birthday to me after school. I wish I was home for my birthday. Mum makes one big spice cake with seven-minute frosting for everyone's birthday at Easter. My dad and Jimmy put quarters, nickels and dimes in the cake, and you get to keep whatever you find in your slice.

Dorothy used to poke around and find out where the quarters were, and take that piece. And she used to dig out the soft part of a fresh loaf of bread Mum just baked and eat all the inside, leaving just the crust. Mum had to throw the crust out to the chickens. It's a good thing Mum bakes lots of loaves.

For my birthday Dorothy bought a home permanent and permed my hair on Saturday. The seniors are allowed to walk to town on every second

Saturday of the month. They have to be back by five o'clock. Dorothy got back by two o'clock so she said she would do my hair, otherwise Sister Theo was going to give me a junior girl haircut again. After Dorothy gave me the perm she combed it a little. Then she started to laugh. Right away I knew that it wasn't going to look beautiful after all. I asked for a mirror. When I saw all the frizz I almost cried. Dorothy cut some off and it looked better, but it's still pretty bad.

Saturday afternoon is like a day off. After we finish scrubbing and polishing floors in the morning we have free time until suppertime, six o'clock. We have to make sure to polish our brown oxford shoes or saddle oxfords which are black and white. Then we have to iron our Sunday clothes and curl our hair with bobby pins or curlers. We put kerchiefs over the curlers. Some girls pluck their eyebrows and shave their legs.

One Saturday last year when she was still an intermediate, Dorothy decided to shave my legs. I didn't want her to because my leg hair was light coloured and didn't even show. Somebody said when you shave your legs once you have to do it for the rest of your life because the hairs get thick and black after that. I asked Dorothy not to shave my legs, but she just laughed and talked me into it. Then she shaved my arms. Finally she shaved my face. I was worried sick that I would start growing a beard. But I didn't. The leg hairs aren't too dark either, but they're darker than before.

I don't like being thirteen very much. Just after Mum talked to me about becoming a woman, sure enough it happened on the first Saturday I was back at school. I felt really unhappy until Cookie said it happens to all girls. The worst part was that I had to ask Sister Theo for pads. When other girls asked, she gave them a dozen, but when I asked she gave me four. Then I had to ask her three or four times. And my cramps were so bad that I wished I were dead.

Thursday, January 22, 1959 *K.I.R.S.*

IT'S really cold out. The floor was so frozen this morning Sister let us kneel on our beds for prayers. There are ice flowers on the windows. It reminds me of the time my dad and Jimmy were listening to the Joe Louis fight on the radio. Missy and I were kneeling on Jimmy's bed playing with the ice flowers on the window. We melted them with our breath and moved them around the window like boats. Jimmy got mad and put Missy outside because she was laughing too loud. Then she was crying at the window, looking in. I yelled, "Don't worry, they'll let you in soon." Then my dad got mad and put me outside too. Missy kept quiet after that because she wasn't scared anymore. Mum came and let us in. She was frowning at Jimmy and my dad.

When we are at home we have to pack water from the well. One night my dad told us to pack snow in buckets to put into the tub on the stove. We all went outside, and it was really cold. The snow was sparkling on the ground, and there must have been a million stars out. Dorothy showed us the Milky Way. Then my dad told Jimmy about flying saucers. He said someone in Scotland saw one. We all looked up thinking maybe we'd see one because the sky was so clear. Missy and I got scared and ran in the house. We screamed, then started laughing.

Benny was born in the winter, in December, when I was seven. I thought he was a kitten mewing. Then my mum told me to climb over the bed and look. There he was. His mouth was round. He was crying. I asked Mum where he came from. She said God gave the baby to her. I asked her if God put clothes on the baby first. She didn't say.

She said it was a good thing I kept going into her room before Benny was born because she was almost going to pass out when she had him. Just me and Missy were home. Missy was sleeping. When my dad came home he went and got Dr. Benjamin. That's why my dad named the baby Benjamin.

Mum kept telling me to go pack some water in my lard pail. My dad put a string on it so I can throw it in the well and get water like Jimmy. He packs water in big buckets every day.

We got in trouble over that lard pail one time. Missy put it on her head like a hat. Then she put it on me. "Let's put it on the baby," we said. We put it on Benny's head but then it fell over his face. He started to howl. Nobody could get it off. Finally my dad had to get a tool that looks like big scissors and cut it off. My dad got mad and put us in the meat-house where he hangs the deer meat. We looked out the cracks and watched the chickens.

Not long after Benny was born Dorothy came home. My dad drove over to Kalamak to get her, and they came home late at night. The first thing Dorothy wanted to do was see the baby. She saw Missy sleeping on Mum's bed and said, "Gee, the baby's big." Next day Dorothy told me that the baby came out of Mum's tummy.

Sunday, January 25, 1959 K.I.R.S.

WE went to perform at the Snow Festival in Vernon this weekend. We loaded up our suitcases and costume boxes and left Kalamak at nine o'clock Saturday morning on a chartered bus. It was nice and warm. Our old yellow school bus is cold. It smells of diesel.

I sat beside Missy and we played cat's cradle for

awhile, until I got too bus sick. Then I stared out the window and fell asleep. I woke up once to hear the rumble of the bus motor and the sound of the kids talking and laughing. I do not know how anyone can talk and laugh on a bus. I felt like jumping into ice-cold water to clear my head.

I looked at Missy. She was playing Old Maid with her friend Patsy across the aisle, and chewing spearmint gum. The smell of the gum made my stomach turn. I turned my face to the window and went back to sleep.

When I woke up again, at noon, we were pulling into Vernon. Sister Theo handed out peanut butter sandwiches and pop. Then she told us we could walk down main street and watch the parade. We had to come back to the bus at four o'clock and wait to be picked up for our performance.

I climbed out of the bus feeling green and dizzy. I liked the cold air. I stumbled after the other girls as they walked in a group towards main street. Then the group split and I didn't know which one to follow. I decided to go with Missy and her friends. We kept walking and walking in the snow until we realized we weren't getting to main street. We were cold by then and we didn't know where to go. We didn't know how to get back to the bus.

Finally one of the girls said she knew where the Sisters' convent was, just up the street. We followed her and rang on the doorbell. A nun opened the door and we explained who we were. She let us in and told us to stay in the living room. Then she left. We stayed there for a long time. We were hungry and thirsty, but at least we were warm.

At about four-thirty we heard the rumble of the bus outside and we ran out to join the other dancers. Dorothy said the parade had been just wonderful with clowns, floats, bands, and best of all the queens like Miss Vernon, Miss Kamloops and Miss Kelowna. They wore fancy coats and tiaras that look like shiny crowns.

The bus driver brought us to an old hall where some ladies made us a dinner of chicken, mashed potatoes, mixed vegetables, buns and jello. When we finished eating we went by bus to the high school to get ready to perform. While we were waiting for Sister Theo to get the key to the change room, we walked around the school halls looking at pictures of graduating classes.

Then we changed into our first set of costumes, fixed our hair and put on make-up. Sister Superior came and put eye drops into our eyes to make them shiny on stage. She told us to do our best, and to smile, smile, smile.

And we did.

It is always exciting to put on a concert. I like the smell of the ironed costumes, the colourful look of the folk dances, the sound of the applause when it keeps going for a long time.

Afterwards, we packed up our costumes, washed the make-up off our faces and lined up to get our billets.

Missy and I got to stay with a couple called Mr. and Mrs. Backan. He's an undertaker. They had a fancy new house with frilly yellow curtains and beige rugs. They had new tables and chairs, a new chesterfield, new everything. The room they gave us was so spotless. I was scared to ruin it so I slept on the floor.

In the morning Mrs. Backan went to church and Mr. Backan made us toast with poached eggs. We had never seen poached eggs before. They looked so small on the toast, like eyes. Missy and I looked at each other and we started to giggle. Mr. Backan didn't say a word. He looked at us as if he had never seen girls laugh before. After that we tried to make conversation like Sister Theo told us. But Mr. Backan didn't seem to want to talk. Some people who billet us ask all kinds of questions, mostly who taught us to dance and sing. Some people seem to like us.

After breakfast Mr. Backan drove us to the church for second Mass, then we boarded the bus and came back.

BROTHER Reilly talked to me about writing today. He's the grade seven teacher. He was reading our stories on the bulletin board in the library when we were taking books out. He called me over to talk about my legend.

He spoke very quietly so no one could hear. "You're very talented in writing," he said. "This story on the ghost horse is rich in imagery. I think you should consider writing seriously some day. Maybe in your forties. Then you'll have some sense. In the meantime keep journals and write to penpals. I'd like you to illustrate this story and we'll put it on the bulletin board in the hall. All right?" I nodded and sat down again. I pretended to read but I couldn't think for a long time. A golden feeling kept washing over me.

Writing is something I love to do. Maybe it's because I never know what to say to people, except for my family. When I write a story the words just keep coming and coming from some place inside of me.

I don't usually get good marks. Teachers are always looking for punctuation and spelling and grammar. They tell us to write on topics I don't care about. The only trouble with writing is that nothing interesting ever happens to me. Maybe when I'm older I'll be shipwrecked and find a treasure or travel to another galaxy or something.

Brother Reilly has health posters of Indian people on his class walls. They encourage people to drink lots of water and eat healthy food. We heard when he teaches art, he doesn't mind if students use Indian designs. Sometimes he's sarcastic though. He'll say to us girls, "Come on, beauties, it's time for class." We have pimples and we're clumsy, and we blush all the time. We say stupid things.

One time after reading an English novel I spoke with an English accent for a couple of days. Brother Reilly acted the same as usual but his eyes were kind of smiling. Maybe that's what he was thinking about when he said I might have some sense when I'm in my forties.

After class some of the girls asked me what Brother Reilly said to me. "He just wants me to draw a picture of my horse story for the bulletin board," I told them. I didn't want Edna finding out what he said to me about my writing. She'd twist my arm and ask me if I thought I was smart.

Thursday, February 12, 1959 K.I.R.S.

I GOT chicken pox at the square dance jamboree last Saturday. Some of us dancers went there to perform.

We do that to earn money for service clubs or church committees.

There's forty of us, from grade one to twelve. Sister Theo teaches us the folk dances. Sister Theo and Sister Superior come from Ireland. Sister Superior teaches us to sing Irish songs. We learn these songs and folk dances for the Irish concert, and also the music festival. That's what we were doing at the square dance jamboree, performing.

I usually do the Sailor's Hornpipe and the Highland Fling and Irish Jig. Sister makes us smile all the time we are dancing. If we don't she punches us on the back or hits us with the shilayley. That's an Irish walking stick, and I don't know how to spell it. Once she threw an apple at one of the dancers and she missed. We all felt like laughing but we didn't dare. She got really mad then and somebody got a licking. Dorothy told me once that one of the senior girls got tired of being punched so she grabbed Sister's arms and held them down. Sister told her to kneel but she wouldn't. Finally Sister told her she was a good girl, and then she let go. Sister didn't pick on her anymore after that. The way Sister Theo yells at us reminds me of my dad when he's drinking. It scares me.

Sometimes I hate being a dancer. Sister Theo just called me one day and told me I was to be a dancer. We have no play time. The other girls hate us because they say we are Sister's pets. The worst thing is that the audience can see our bloomers when we dance because Sister makes us lift our legs high. One of the boys told Edna that after we performed for the whole school. Edna said all the boys were laughing at us.

We left for the jamboree right after school. We didn't get to eat until after the performance. When we got back to the school at midnight we changed into our smocks and went down to the kitchen for cookies and powdered milk. We call those cookies dog biscuits because they have no sugar in them.

I was just standing there feeling dizzy when Sister Superior came in. She said, "What's the matter with Martha? Her cheeks look flushed." She stood behind me looking down my back and said, "Look, there are red bumps popping out all over her back." She laughed as she watched them pop out. Then Sister Theo sent me right to bed.

I'm glad Sister Superior was there. That time I caught the flu Sister Theo yelled at me and kept punching me on the back until I almost fell. Once she punched me and I got a boil on my back. I was scared to tell her, so I didn't.

I like Sister Nurse, though. She looks after the first-aid room. She is old. Her eyebrows are white and her eyes are shiny. When she talks her i's sound like ee's. She's French, that's why. She tells us about Juneau, Alaska. She was there before. I'm the only intermediate who got chicken pox. Three junior girls got it too.

Sunday, February 15, 1959 *K.I.R.S.*

This morning everybody got up and went to Mass, but Sister told me to stay in bed because I still have my spots. It's quiet in the dorm with everybody gone.

Usually, the only time in my life when it's quiet is when I am home. Not inside the house, but in the hills above our ranch. My dad saddles up Baldy and lets me ride him into the hills any time I ask. Sometimes I sing a song. Sometimes I just listen to the quiet as we ride along. Baldy's bridle jingles a little and the saddle squeaks. Spud comes along too. He's a police dog, a German shepherd.

He kind of dances as he steps along, Baldy. He's a sorrel gelding, my dad's saddle horse. He's a good hunting horse because he doesn't get jumpy when my dad takes a shot on his back. When he sees a deer he keeps really still, just watching until my dad sees. Same with Spud.

My dad's a hunter. He rides into the hills above our ranch early in the morning before the sun is up. He shoots a deer and brings it home on Baldy. Then my mum cuts up the meat and cooks it or cans it in

Mason jars. My parents take meat to old people when we visit.

Baldy has some bad habits. He likes to run away with you if he thinks he can get away with it. He jumps fences when he does, and sometimes he gallops under low-hanging branches to knock you off. He ran away with me once and I whipped him. He pulls the bridle in his teeth and runs for the barn. I just pull on one rein until his head is twisted around and he can't see. Then he behaves. He hasn't tried to buck me off since I whipped him.

Once Cookie and I decided to pick saskatoon berries on his back because the bushes were tall. I was in the saddle facing Baldy's head. Cookie was behind me facing his tail so she could reach the berries better.

Suddenly a coyote jumped out of the bushes and ran for the fence. Baldy flung up his head and I lost the reins. Then he turned and raced for home.

As he galloped full speed across the field, Cookie screamed, "Tootie, stop the horse, I'm riding backwards."

"I can't," I yelled. "I dropped the reins."

"I'm falling off," she shrieked.

"Grab onto the thongs on the saddle!"

Cookie kept yelling, "Halp, halp, halp," but she stayed on all the way to the barn. When Baldy put the brakes on she flipped off backwards and rolled over and bumped her head on the barn door. She screwed up her eyes and bawled, holding her head. That was the last time she ever rode with me.

Thursday, February 26, 1959 *K.I.R.S.*

SISTER Superior told Mr. Oiko this morning that she was taking me to town. Sisters are not allowed to go anywhere by themselves. I liked going with her because we talked about things. She asked me what I'm learning in math and other subjects, mostly school stuff. She drove to somewhere in town, to a back yard and parked. I stayed in the car when she went in to visit. She never talked about it when we drove back to the school. I never asked her.

When I am home I go places with my dad. He goes to people's houses and talks to them in Indian for a long time. Usually it's to help people with the land or the law. He says Indians might get to vote soon, so they talk about the different political parties that might help the Indians. My dad's a court interpreter. He speaks six Indian languages.

When I get tired of listening I go outside to see what kind of stock they have, usually some horses and cows, and always a dog. I make friends with the dogs by whining just like a real dog. They look at me and tilt their heads from side to side as if they are trying to hear better. After that they like me and don't bark or try to bite.

The best part of any visit is the horses. I pull out some grass to feed them and rub their ears. I talk to them. Sometimes they perk up their ears as if they understand every word. Other times they put their ears back and nudge me because they want more grass, not conversation.

Some horses are really smart, like Baldy. My dad calls him John W. Baldy, and laughs. Baldy knows how to open slipwire gates, especially if he's on the way home. He nudges them with his nose and they fall open. The trouble is that he can't be bothered waiting for you to climb down, close the gate again and climb back on. If he can get away with it, he'll yank the reins away from you and gallop home.

If it's a pole gate he knows how to stand really close to it so you can reach it to open it. Then he walks through slowly so you can close the gate on the other side.

Once Dorothy and I were riding double and I jumped off to close the slipwire. Baldy tossed his head and took off like a shot for home, with Dorothy hollering and hanging on for dear life. You could see his dust trail for half an hour after that.

Baldy has a sense of humour too. We were all trying to catch him once, about a dozen of us. He kept galloping circles around us with his tail in the air and his head high. My brother Jimmy roped him and got dragged about thirty feet before giving up.

Finally Baldy must have got tired so he galloped once more around us all and stopped short right in front of Dorothy, nose to nose. Dorothy looked away first. Baldy didn't move until Jimmy came and put a halter on him.

I love horses. They are so free. I draw pictures of them all the time, in my notebooks, in art class, on scrap paper, even once for the class bulletin board. Mostly my horses are galloping headlong somewhere, or rearing up.

Sunday, March 8, 1959 K.I.R.S.

AFTER lunch today Sister Theo took us for a walk out to the highway. We do that every Sunday. We line up two by two and walk to the highway and back, or down along the river. When we walked past the river Cookie told Sister that her rubbers were hurting her feet. She was really limping, but Sister just got mad at her and told her to get back in line. When we got back to the school Cookie's feet were bleeding. The girls crowded around to have a look. She was trying not to cry but the tears were rolling down her cheeks. Sister took her to the first-aid room.

Poor Cookie. Last year when she was still a junior that mean Sister Adela who got sent away kicked her down the stairs. The junior girls were late for breakfast and Sister Adela went up to find out why. They were standing in line at the top of the stairs waiting for her to lead them, because that's the rule. Sister Adela got mad and started shoving and pushing the girls to make them hurry. That's when she kicked Cookie. Lucky she fell on some girls who were running ahead of her.

I heard that Sister Adela got mad at the frogs too. Sometimes when it's almost summer the frogs start singing really loud all night. It's because we're next to the river and frogs like water. Anyway, Sister Adela couldn't get to sleep with all the frogs making such a ruckus. She came stomping out of her room, opened up one of the dorm windows and told the frogs to shut up. Of course they didn't. That's when Sister Adela took off her shoes and threw them out the window at the frogs. She was screaming at them. A few days after that, Sister Superior came and told the junior girls that Sister Adela was going away and Sister Claire would take her place.

I like frogs myself. When they sing it makes me think of Loon Lake. My dad took us fishing there one Easter. We were all sitting around the campfire on stumps eating trout that Mum cooked on a frying pan. Suddenly Dorothy screamed and ran a few steps away from her seat. "What is it?" asked Mum. Dorothy pointed to a frog on the ground. Jimmy laughed and laughed at her for being afraid of a frog.

Later our truck got stuck in the mud. We had to

stay overnight and it got really cold. We had one big quilt that me and my sisters and Benny cuddled up under, next to Mum. We made a mattress out of fir boughs. My dad made a big camp fire. He and Jimmy stayed near the fire all night, and they kept checking the fish net in the lake. Towards morning I got really cold so I went and joined them for awhile. They were talking about hunting.

"You cold?" said Dad. I nodded. He gave me some coffee with lots of sugar and canned milk. I warmed my hands over the fire, then my back, just like my dad, looking up at the stars

Thursday, March 12, 1959 *K.I.R.S.*

THE wind was cold again today. It reminded me of what Sister Cecilia told us in grade two, that in March the March winds blow. She said April showers bring May flowers. I wish she was still my teacher. She smiled and laughed a lot. I think she liked us.

When I was in grade two Sister Superior came to our class one day and took Charlie and me away. Charlie likes me, but he didn't come back to school this year. In grade one he rolled an orange across the table at me. I rolled it back.

Sister Superior told me and Charlie that we were skipping grade two and going into grade three, Miss Finny's class. Cookie told me later that the grade two class was too crowded, that's why we had to leave. Cookie stayed in grade two that year. That's why it's hard to be best friends with her. We go to different classrooms now.

I didn't like it in grade three. On my first day, Miss Finny made me go to the blackboard and showed me how to write. She got mad when I couldn't write "f" the right way. She grabbed the chalk out of my hand and hollered at me. She made me do it until I got it right. Then a boy named Timmy pushed my seat up when I went to sit down. I sat on the floor, and everybody laughed. Tears came to my eyes because it really hurt. But I wouldn't let them see.

In the dining room after supper I went to see Dorothy and I told her Miss Finny was mean to me. Dorothy said, that's nothing. She said in grade three she had Miss Finny for a teacher. Miss Finny used to kneel behind her desk and drink something out of a brown paper bag. They could see the bag come up over the top of the desk. Then Miss Finny would stand up and ask the grade threes if they loved her. "YASS, MISS FINNY," they sang all together. Then she gave them each a candy.

I guess grade three wasn't so bad after all. I liked it when Miss Finny asked me to stand up in front of the class and sing Oh Dear What Can the Matter Be. Besides, Sister Cecilia goes to the bathroom. I heard her when I had the flu that time. She thought I was

72

sleeping when she came out of her room. Then she went right into the girls' bathroom and went. I could not believe my ears.

Thursday, March 19, 1959 K.I.R.S.

SISTER Theo is all excited about the Irish concert. She stomped into the rec with a big smile on her face today, and told us we are the last ones on the program. It's the best place to be. The concert is in two days to celebrate St. Patrick's Day, at St. Mark's School in town. We started practising in September and now it's almost here. After that will be the music festival. Dancers, singers and choirs from all over the district will come and compete for top marks.

This year my group has learned how to do the Fairy Reel, an Irish dance with fancy foot work. We do square, line and star patterns as we are dancing. We have to keep straight backs and lift our legs high to do it well. And smile, of course. We wear green kilts with big silver pins, white satin shirts, black sequined boleros, black dance slippers and green hats.

Other dances we younger kids do are the Sailor's Hornpipe, the Highland Fling and the Dutch Tulip Dance. The older girls do a Ukrainian dance, a garland dance, the tarantella which is an Italian dance, a Mexican dance, a Danish dance, a Spanish dance and other Irish dances.

The concert we put on is like a variety show. We sing, dance, do choral speaking and some dialogue, which is talking. There are forty of us girls picked out by Sister Theo and Sister Superior. Some dress up like boys, but we all wear make-up like rouge for our cheeks, eyebrow pencil, mascara, blue eye shadow and bright red lipstick.

We sing a lot of Irish songs in the concert. We harmonize in alto, tenor and soprano. We practise so much on Sunday afternoons that I sometimes almost fall asleep on my feet, and my whole body aches. If somebody sings off-key, Sister Superior keeps us singing until she finds out who it is. Then she makes them practise over and over alone until they get it on key. She makes us sing warm-ups and octaves over and over at the beginning. Do, re, mi, fa, so, la, ti, do. Do, ti, la, so, fa, me, re, do. She hits the piano key hard to make sure we have it right. When Sister Superior says good, you know she means it.

I like singing. Sometimes at home my dad asks us girls to sing a song. We usually sing something like Ho Ro My Nut Brown Maiden or Bless This House that Sister Superior taught us, in harmony. Other times when we're tired walking back from the river we hold hands and march in time to cadet songs Jimmy sings, like Rocky Mountain Rangers. The best is the one I call the tree song. When I'm in the hills alone on Baldy I sing a song with no words. It sounds like a bird call, a little like a laugh that goes into the trees and comes back in an echo. It's like the trees are answering me. That's why I call it the tree song.

Thursday, March 26, 1959   K.I.R.S.

THE Irish concert is over and we were in the news. It was written in big letters on the second page of the Kalamak News on Monday, DANCERS WOW AUDIENCE. There is a photograph of our eight senior girl dancers smiling and doing the Eight Hand Reel in two rows facing each other. There is another picture of two tiny dancers from the ballet dance studio in town doing a Leprechaun dance, and a nice article about the concert. They said the Kalamak Indian Residential School dancers gave a flawless performance in perfect unison and won the hearts of the people. Sister Theo cut it out and saved it in a scrapbook.

It was an interesting evening. We heard another choir sing Irish songs. We watched other dancers from behind the curtains. They did Irish and Scottish dances in costumes like ours. They were nervous and giggly like us but they had white skin and some had blond hair and blue eyes. We didn't make friends until near the end when a few of them talked to some of our dancers.

A girl called Sandra asked us who taught us to dance, and where did we go to school. They were surprised to find out we had to go to an Indian school and stay there all year. They go to public school and get to go home every day when classes are over. They asked what boarding school was like. We told them it was like being in school all day instead of just part of the day. They said they wouldn't like that. We don't either. When Sister Theo saw us talking to them she came over and told us to go back to the dressing room. When we got there she told us not to be wandering around getting in the way. We knew she didn't want us talking to those dancers.

My favourite part of the concert was this song called Danny Boy. I was pulling on my leotards when I heard the most beautiful voice singing a sad song. I dressed quickly and went out to the stage so I could see who it was.

I saw the back of a tall woman with long black curly hair who had her arm stretched out to a young man across the stage in a red uniform. She was singing in a high voice that quivered. I cried at the end when she sang, "Oh Danny boy, oh Danny boy, I love you so." The audience clapped and clapped and clapped.

The woman stood there looking up for a long time. Then she walked over to the centre of the stage and bowed. She held her hand out to the young man and he took it and they turned and bowed together.

I could see then that she was old, maybe in her thirties. The boy looked seventeen. They walked off stage together, and I didn't see them again.

Later there was a play of some kind. It seemed like it had something to do with a football player who got caught up in the sinful ways of the world. I didn't like it because it was too much like a bawling out.

Thursday, April 2, 1959 K.I.R.S

FATHER Sloane came to the girls' rec yesterday to tease us about April Fool's Day. He said you can't choose your own face but you can pick your own nose. I don't know why that is so funny. He comes every day almost, for a few minutes. Once he told me that my name Martha comes from the Bible. Martha was a friend of Jesus. I don't like my white name much. It's not very pretty.

My dad gave me my Indian name, Seepeetza. I was named after an old lady who died a long time ago. My dad laughs sometimes when he says my name, because it means White Skin or Scared Hide. It's a good name for me because I get scared of things, like devils.

My dad called me Tootie first, when I was really small. We were sitting at the table having tea, and he was teaching me some words. Say pass the spoon, he said to me. I said pass the spoot, and he laughed and laughed. Then he started calling me Toot McSpoot, and everybody at home calls me Toot or Tootie now. My dad still calls me McSpoot. He's the only one.

We all have Indian names but we're not allowed to use them at school. Jimmy is Kyep-kin, Coyote Head, because he sings a lot. Dorothy is Qwileen meaning Birch Tree because she worries about the trees. Missy is Kekkix meaning Mouse Hands and Benny is Hop-o-lox-kin. I don't know what that means. We don't use our Indian names much. My parents know we would get in trouble at school if we used them there.

Benny got his name from an old lady called Mathilda. She asked Mum what she was going to call that little boy. Mum said she was going to call him Toyax-kin, because he runs all over the hills. Old Mathilda said she should call him Hop-o-lox-kin after her grandfather, because my dad is her relative. Then she took a quarter out of her pocket. She said she was going to give that quarter to Benny and if he took it then his name was going to be Hop-o-lox- kin. Sure enough he took it and then he got his name.

All the old Indian people know our Indian names, our white names and our nicknames. They know all about us.

The old timers call my little sister Missy Poison. When she was a little girl she used to mix all her food in one bowl, then turn it upside down over her head.

She almost ate a spider once too. It was a popcorn spider that came down from the ceiling in the verandah onto her baby walker. Mum came out and saw the legs in her hand and washed it off.

Yay-yah says not to kill spiders or there will be a thunderstorm. She said a long time ago it was Skokki the Spider who travelled to the moon and learned from the sky dwellers how to weave. That's why our people have baskets. My mum's grandmother used to make baskets out of cedar roots and chokecherry bark. Mum doesn't make baskets. She collects medicine tea from the mountains, and Yay-yah makes things like moccasins out of buckskin. Moccasins are like slippers.

Thursday, April 9, 1959 K.I.R.S.

I WENT to see the dentist. He looked at my teeth and said I needed seven fillings. I got really scared. Cookie said that fillings are the worst because you sometimes have to get a needle in your mouth. It's called freezing. She said it hurts worse if you don't get the needle. The dentist doesn't believe in freezing, but if kids start screaming he gives it to them in their gums.

Mr. Oiko sent some of us to the nurse's room. We sat on chairs outside and listened to the kids crying and screaming in there, and something that sounded like a sewing machine. We could hear a man's voice snarling. One of the kids whispered that he slapped a grade five girl because she turned her head away and broke the needle in her mouth. One of the grade twos came out holding her mouth with blood seeping through a white bandage and rolling down her chin. She was crying, and she wouldn't look at us.

Then it was my turn, and I felt like I had a bellyache. The dentist looked at me and told me to sit in this big chair that moved up and down. He was holding a needle. He put it down and made me open my mouth. He looked around my mouth with a little mirror on a little silver handle. He poked at my teeth with a silver tool. His hand smelled like soap. He had on thick glasses, and he was really big. He growled, "Get your TONGUE out of the way." Everything he said was like a growl. Move your HEAD back. Don't close your MOUTH. Keep STILL. OPEN YOUR MOUTH!

When he said I had to get seven fillings I thought I was going to get them done right away, and I felt like my blood was draining from my body.

Then he told me to leave and come back the next day. I had a bellyache all night. I couldn't sleep. I didn't want to eat. It reminded me of a book I read called *A Tale of Two Cities*. This guy Charles Darnay knew he was going to the guillotine the next day to get his head chopped off. That's how I felt.

This time when I went to the dentist at least I was ready. I sat in the chair and held onto the chair sides until my hands and arms and neck ached while he drilled my teeth. That drill sounded like a scream. At first it didn't hurt. Then it felt like a hot knife, and I started to groan and he pulled the drill out. Then he heated up some metal and pushed it into the hole he made. He made big ones, and now my teeth are all ugly.

I couldn't believe I needed seven fillings because they said you only have to get fillings if your teeth are partly rotten or have black dots on them. Mine were all white, except for one small dot. Cookie says the dentist gets so much money for each filling and each tooth he pulls. He takes them out with a tool that looks like a pair of pliers.

Thursday, April 16, 1959 K.I.R.S

SISTER Theo always gets cranky on Monday, laundry day. Every other Monday we have to take our bottom sheets, pillowcases, towels, facecloths, bloomers and undershirts and put them into baskets to be taken to the laundry in the basement.

We have to work on laundry day too. The older girls handle the washers and dryers and mangle which presses the sheets. Two of us stand at the end and fold sheets as they come off the mangle. Sometimes I press clothes or fold clothes as they come out of the dryers. Later we darn socks.

One thing I like is that two of us get to carry the basket of clean socks to the boys' side. It's the only time we're allowed to go there. It looks just like the girls' side. We like to see which boys are around, and whether they smile at us.

In the afternoon we go to class but before we do Sister lines us up and tells us that she has been slaving like a black in the laundry room for us for thirteen years. She calls us ungrateful wretches and sly-puss, boy crazy, amathons. I don't know what amathon means, maybe like female warriors along the Amazon River.

Sister Theo must get tired. She is the supervisor for ninety-nine intermediate girls, the biggest group in school. That means she has to get us up and ready for Mass, line us up for breakfast, give us all jobs to do after breakfast, make sure we get to class on time, make us change into smocks after school, hand out apples. She has to make sure we do our homework, take our baths, brush our teeth and change our sheets. She's also in charge of the dancers, the costumes, the out-of-town trips. I heard Father Sloane say once that Sister is like a sergeant major, always yelling orders. She told Father he was a scream. Those Irish talk to each other like that. They insult each other, then laugh and laugh.

I told Dorothy I hated Sister Theo because she

gave me the strap for forgetting my towel downstairs. My mum and dad never hit us. Then Dorothy told me all those things Sister has to do. She said the Sisters have to get up at five o'clock in the morning to say prayers. I wasn't mad anymore.

I still don't like Sister Theo, though. Once she came into my tub room when I was going to have my bath. She told me to get my clothes off and get in the water. I wouldn't. I will not let anyone see me without my clothes on. When she yelled at me to take my bloomers off and get in the tub I looked at the DANGER sign up where the electricity switches are. She saw it too. I was thinking if she made me do it I would wait till she left, climb up on the pipe, touch the switch and get electrocuted. We stared at each other. Then she opened the door and went out.

I took my bloomers off and climbed in the tub. My hands were shaking for a long time. We're not supposed to look at the Sisters like that.

Thursday, April 23, 1959 K.I.R.S.

I SAW St. Joseph last night. I think it was him because he wore a brown robe like St. Joseph in the holy picture of Baby Jesus and the Virgin Mary. That St. Joseph was old with white hair but the one I talked to last night had long dark hair and looked younger.

At first when I woke up it was dark, and I couldn't

see him very well. I woke up when he put his hand on my arm. It was warm. It felt like he knew me, like we were best friends. He smiled and said my real name, Seepeetza.

I asked him how come I had to get into trouble so much. In class I get in trouble for daydreaming. In the rec Edna wants to beat me up because I have green eyes. White people don't like us because our clothes are old. Sister clobbers me for making dancing mistakes. The worst is that I get scared to walk to the bathroom in the dark. In the morning I feel just sick when Sister yells at me and hits me and makes me wear my wet sheet over my head in front of everybody.

St. Joseph looked right into my eyes and told me that I had to learn humility, that it was really important. He held me close, and I fell asleep.

When I woke up again, Sister was ringing the bell. I checked my bed. It was dry. I was so happy. I slid off the bed onto my knees. We all said our morning prayers, the Our Father, Hail Mary and Glory Be. I didn't tell anyone about my dream, but I was happy all day.

Sister told us about St. Joseph. He was humble because he looked after Mary and Jesus even though Jesus wasn't his own son. He was a carpenter. I think that's true because his hand was calloused like my dad's. My dad works hard on the ranch.

I'm not very humble. I know this because my

mum said I have a temper like my dad. Once we were walking in front of the boys on our way to class when Father Sloane came along and picked me up, laughing. When he threw me over his shoulder, my skirt flew up and the whole class saw my bloomers. My bloomers were inside out because Sister made us hurry too fast in the morning. All the boys except Charlie laughed at me. I got so mad that I decided to sharpen my pencil and stab Father Sloane with it if he did that again.

If I was humble I wouldn't have been so mad. I think St. Joseph knows that. That's why he came. I guess what I want most in the world is for someone to like me, to be my best friend. Nobody wants to be friends with someone who looks like a shamah. Even Cookie avoids me most of the time. I miss my mum. I miss her all the time. When St. Joseph came he showed me lots of friends, maybe a million that I will have one day. They were reaching out to shake my hand. The trouble is I was really old. Over twenty, I think.

Thursday, April 30, 1959 K.I.R.S.

I KEEP thinking about my dream of St. Joseph. You can tell he likes children. He understands about things. Like what Sister told us about devils dragging us into hell if we sin.

During the day I'm not afraid of devils but at night when the lights go out an awful thing happens. I feel like I'm falling into a huge black hole where the devils are waiting, laughing. They are really horrible. Big. I feel sweat on my face but I'm cold. I take tiny breaths so they won't hear me. They stay under my bed all night waiting for me to make a mistake or breathe too loud. I stay awake sometimes until it starts getting light outside.

After I saw St. Joseph I felt like someone was looking out for me. I was still scared of the devils but I got up anyway and tiptoed to the bathroom really quiet. I kept hearing creaks behind me but I wouldn't look. The hair at the back of my head prickled. When I got to the bathroom I switched the light on really fast. It took me along time to go back to bed because I was scared to turn off the bathroom light again.

I'm still scared of the devils. I still can't sleep for a long time at night or let my hands or feet go over the edge of the bed, but at least now my bed is dry.

Sister told us about sin in catechism class. She said we sin when we lie or cheat or steal or skip Mass on Sunday, eat meat on Friday, kill, or curse, or argue, or call names, or even think bad thoughts. She said everybody sins every day, at least seven times. If we die without confessing small sins, then we will go to purgatory. If we die in a state of mortal sin we go to hell. You can pray people out of purgatory but never out of hell.

But what about Sister? She's not nice. I don't think St. Joseph liked it that I was so angry at Sister. He said Sisters are poor things sometimes too. He said to keep my eyes on my own heart. What a funny thing to say.

Once I stole a pair of socks from Edna. Somebody stole my socks and I think it was her because she hates me. She holds her fist up to my nose all the time. Edna told Sister Theo that I stole her socks but Sister didn't believe her.

We have to wash our socks every night before we go to bed and hang them on the iron bar above our pillows beside our towels and facecloths. Next morning my socks were gone, and there was an ugly pair there instead. Somebody usually steals my comb and my toothpaste, probably Edna. Then I have to borrow a comb and brush my teeth with baking soda. It tastes ugly. Sometimes Cookie and I get so hungry at night we eat her toothpaste. It tastes like peppermint candy.

Saturday, May 6, 1959 K.I.R.S.

I NEVER thought I could be happy here at school, but who'd have thought Father Sloane would get us a swimming pool. It's made of cement with a deep end and a shallow end and two diving boards. It's aqua. The water tastes like bleach.

This afternoon after we got our ironing done Sister said we could go swimming. She handed out red bathing suits. I put mine on and went out to the pool with my towel. The water was ice-cold, but I didn't mind. I love swimming as much as I love riding and art.

We just got to stay in the pool for a few minutes. Then we had to go inside, because it was the boys' turn. We looked out the windows and watched them because the pool is just below the girls' side. Sister Delores was watching them too, from one of our dorm windows. Some of the girls snickered about that. A nun watching boys.

At home we go swimming at Big Rock in the Calico River. It's about half a mile from our ranch. We walk or sometimes my dad takes us there on the horses after we get the haying done for the day, or he drives us in his pickup truck. He tells Mum to pack a picnic lunch of sweet tea, tea biscuits, homemade butter, wild strawberry jam or huckleberry jam, and slices of cold roast deer meat, or baloney.

Sometimes my dad takes his spear to catch fish. It has three prongs with a long pole. He watches for a long time where there are logs and branches in the river with the spear ready. Then he plunges the spear into the water. He catches trout that way.

Once Mum made a fish trap out of willow switches and twine. She put it in a place where the fish like to rest, under some branches. Her grandmother, Yetko, taught her how to do this when she was just a little girl. Mum says Yetko taught her everything. She was her friend. Yetko saddled up her little horse and took my mother into the hills to pick wild onions, wild celery, flower tea and all kinds of berries. That's how Mum learned about Indian medicine. They would camp up there alone, sometimes for a week. They never took weapons. My mom said the animals never hurt them.

Mum still knows all about which plants can cure sicknesses. She makes tea out of dried honeysuckle flowers or willow bark to cure headaches. For stomach aches she makes wild strawberry tea. For woman trouble she makes Labrador tea. For really bad sickness she gives a tea made out of deer root. It smells and tastes awful but it cures you. It's strange to think my mum was a little girl, but I saw a picture of her when she was fourteen. She was so tiny.

My mum only went to grade three. She went to Kalamak too. The nuns strapped her all the time for speaking Indian, because she couldn't speak English. She said just when the welts on her hands and arms healed, she got it again. That's why she didn't want us to learn Indian. When Mum and Dad want to talk without us understanding them, they speak Indian. It sounds soft and gentle, like the wind in pines.

SOMETIMES the boys climb Osprey Mountain, not far from the school. We can see them from the dorm and hear them whooping like Indians in the movies. The Indians in the movies are not like anyone I know. Real Indians are just people like anyone else except they love the mountains.

At the end of summer at home we pack up our tent, lots of food, warm winter clothes, all our picking baskets, cooking gear and warm quilts. Then we head up into the mountains to Tekameen Summit. The whole family climbs into the pickup truck and away we go.

When we get up there we pitch the tent, and Mum cooks supper over the campfire. Then we sit around the campfire in the dark and tell stories. My dad tells the best ones, about bears, his war stories and funny things that happen to people. One of his favourites is about the bar in England that wouldn't let you in unless you were a Scot and had Mac in front of your name. One guy tried to get in by saying his name was Macaroni. My dad laughed and laughed and thumped his leg when he told that story.

We camp up there until we fill all our baskets with shiny almost black huckleberries, the best berries of all. They taste sweet and tart. Mum calls them medicine food. We serve huckleberries when we have important visitors.

Yay-yah usually comes berry-picking with us or with Uncle Tommy and his family or Uncle Willy and his family. We all camp in the same spot so we can visit each other's campfires or share food if the hunters get a deer. They call it a moweech.

Usually other Indian families come berry-picking too, and camp nearby. They tell us all the news of their families and some funny stories. They discuss serious business sometimes too, but they talk in Indian so I don't understand what they are talking about. But you can tell it's important by their voices, the serious looks and the quietness of the people listening.

There is something really special about being mountain people. It's a feeling like you know who you are, and you know each other. You belong to the mountains.

The old people like Yay-yah smile at you and tell you something about the trail you're following or show you how to cover your berries with leaves so they stay fresh. They know where to find the biggest berries and how to cook delicious food over the campfire. They notice how many berries you pick, who sneaks off to go fishing, and what everybody likes to eat. They tease you around the campfire if you don't pick many berries. Next day you pick lots.

Two or three ladies will pick in one spot together and talk and laugh all day. One time Mum and I were picking some nice big berries on the side of a steep

hill. Just as we were heading down to camp I tripped
on a tree root and went rolling and tumbling all the
way down the hill, still holding on to my basket. I
landed on my shoulder with my legs high up in the
air. My mum caught up to me, then started to laugh.
"You saved ALL your berries," she said. She told
everybody about it at the campfire. She said, "Tootie
rolled all the way down a BIG hill, and she didn't
spill ANY BERRIES." Yay-yah turned and looked at
me with a little smile, and Dad chuckled. "Good for
you, McSpoot," he said.

When it rains Yay-yah makes a tiny little fire and
practically sits on it to keep warm. Everybody else
makes big fires. Once, too many people crowded
around Yay-yah's fire so Uncle Tommy had to make
her another one.

The men go out with baskets and guns on horse-
back or on foot. They circle all around the camp and
the picking spots to check for bears before they go.
Sometimes they come back with lots of berries.
Other times they just look the mountain valley over,
or do a bit of hunting. They're very quiet in the
woods. We look up sometimes when we're picking
berries and there they are looking at us, and we never
heard them come.

When they hunt, they get up before dawn to
bathe in a deep pool in the mountain stream. When
they come back from the mountains my dad and
uncles talk to each other in Indian and tell each other

what they saw. There isn't a thing about those mountains they don't know.

Sunday, May 24, 1959 *K.I.R.S.*

TODAY we went to Skiddam Flats. It's the Queen's birthday, and we get to go there this time every year. All the junior, intermediate and high school girls go with our supervisors. Father Sloane came too, to go fishing with us. He usually comes to visit the girls every day after school in the rec. He teases us and tells us jokes. One of the girls lets his cigarette ashes fall in her hands so they won't go on the floor.

Mr. Gorky came and picked us up in the cattle truck, and drove us all up into the hills. He runs the farm part of the school. I was cold and I had a headache, but once I got up there I felt happy. It reminded me of the place my dad takes us fishing in the springtime at home, up at Pothole Lake, near a place called Sugarloaf because it looks like a loaf of bread from far away.

There's cows up there grazing in the hills like at home. They're Herefords like our cows. Last year two of the high school girls got lost. They were from Vancouver, a big city. They never saw a cow before and suddenly they saw one right on the trail in front of them. They didn't know what it was. They screamed and ran into the bushes to hide. So they missed the truck and got left. Father Sloane had to drive back and pick them up.

The first thing I wanted to do today was run up a bare hill I saw. That's what we do at home when my dad takes us out into the hills. But Sister Theo told us to eat our lunch, Freshie and jam sandwiches. She handed out small fish hooks and fishing line. Then she told us to get some sticks to make a fishing pole and walk to the lake to do some fishing.

It was about a mile to the lake. I walked there with Dorothy and Missy and Cookie and Pearl. Father Sloane came with us and talked with Dorothy. Dorothy always knows what to say to people. Me I get so shy, I blush and look down.

When we were almost at the lake we saw a porcupine on the road. It climbed a tree when it saw us, and we stood watching it for awhile. I wondered what my dad would say to the porcupine if he were there. He always says something in Indian to animals. He smiles when he talks to them, or chuckles. They look at him for awhile like they understand what he's saying. Then they walk away slowly, not scared. My dad says that the skunk is the king of beasts because even a grizzly bear will back away from a skunk.

We fished all afternoon. A couple of girls caught trout, but they were really small. They had to throw them back in. I didn't want to fish so I walked along the lake with Missy looking at the wildflowers. After that we held hands and sang Eensy Weensy Spider.

Saturday, May 30, 1959 *K.I.R.S.*

I COULDN'T believe it. Mr. Gorky let me ride his horse Penny. Cookie and I walked by the barn after school to look at his nice bay quarterhorse and he said I could ride her on Saturday. First I had to ask Father Sloane. Sister Theo couldn't very well say no after Father Sloane said yes, but she told me to make sure I got my ironing and laundry done first. As if I could, with a hundred girls and only two irons. I sneaked off right after lunch, hoping to get back in time to do my ironing.

Mr. Gorky saddled up Penny and adjusted the stirrups for me, just like my dad does at home. He told me to ride on the road along the river, and not to gallop Penny too fast.

It was beautiful. Penny is a dainty walker, and she has a sensitive mouth. I walked her for about a mile and back. Then I felt like a good gallop, so I turned her into the orchard where there is a soft dirt road. I nudged her into a trot, then a gallop. Then I kicked her into a race. We thundered past the orchard along the road, which led down a steep bank and up into the field where the river curves right. I pulled on the reins and said, "Whoa!"

I had a hard time getting her back under control. By then she was mad, so I turned her home and brought her past the barn and up towards the mountains. I rode around in the hills all afternoon.

When I got back to the school I was hot and tired, and sure enough I was late for the ironing room. Sister got mad, but I didn't care. The ride was worth it.

Horses are important at home. My dad's a hay contractor, or he was until everybody started getting tractors. He uses team horses for haying. He also needs a saddle horse for hunting and chasing the cattle up to the rangeland.

We used to travel everywhere with horse and buggy, but now Dad has his truck. Lots of people drive cars now, but some people don't, like my Uncle Willy. He comes rolling in to our ranch with his wagon and team horses, and all the family. Sometimes they camp for a week, and other visitors come, Uncle Tommy, Aunt Ella, Yay-yah, Aunt Mamie and Uncle Les. They all have big families. We visit and eat big meals and play with the kids and tell stories. At night the boys sleep outside in the wagons. Everybody else sleeps on the floor. My dad plays his fiddle and Uncle Les plays the guitar and they sing half the night, passing around a mickey. The songs I like best are She'll be Coming Round the Mountain and Forever My Darling. Uncle Tommy cries when he sings it.

We're always sad when the visitors leave. We follow the wagons, waving and waving until they pass the gate and disappear into the trees. Then we go for a walk up into the hills to this place where there is a big stone cliff and fir trees, and a tall jack pine. It's quiet there. When we come back we feel better.

Thursday, June 4, 1959 K.I.R.S.

LAST Saturday one of the boys hanged himself in the tek, where the boys do woodworking. His name was Leo. He was in grade four, so I didn't know him. They say he was playing Zorro with some friends. He hanged himself but someone was supposed to cut him down. The bell rang for supper, and whoever was supposed to rescue him didn't get a chance to go back. We are going to have a special Mass for Leo, but no funeral because he will be buried at home.

Now I found out that Charlie died too. One of the girls from Lillooet told Cookie. It was last summer. He was fishing, and he fell into the Fraser River. At first I didn't believe it. I thought it was just a story. I didn't think I cared, because it was just skinny Charlie with his hair sticking up like a rooster tail at the back. He used to make me cards on St. Valentine's Day. He told Cookie I was his girl. What if no one ever calls me their girl again? What if he was the only one?

I'm glad now that Sister makes us dancers practise and practise for concerts. It helps me forget about Charlie. I don't even mind when she locks me in the linen room to learn folk dances out of books and teach them to the other dancers. She doesn't want anyone to know she's not the dance teacher herself. Dorothy used to do that too when she was an intermediate, but now she's a senior. Cookie said it isn't right for Sister to say she's the dance teacher but I don't care. I just want to keep busy.

I'm kind of mean now too. I told Edna to shut up because she was singing "Chinky Chinky Chinaman, sitting on a fence, trying to make a dollar out of fifteen cents." She used to sing that to Charlie because his eyes slanted up. I don't know why, but I wasn't as scared of her anymore. So I said, "Edna, shut up."

"Make me," she said. Then she ran off laughing. It's the Irish in me that gets so mad, just like Dad. His grandfather was Irish. I know it's not the Indian in me that's mean because Yay-yah is kind and gentle, like Mum. She has no white in her.

Sister Theo is Irish too. She calls the boys those dirty boys.

She talks about the sin of being boy crazy and how it's bad to even think about boys. She says never to get in a car with a boy. When Emma told Sister that her brother got married to a Protestant, Sister bawled her out like it was Emma who married a Protestant.

When we have dances in the gym, we're only allowed to have three dances with the same boy. Once a grade four boy called Peter wrapped his arms around one of the girls and waltzed real close. Sister went marching over and split them up. Peter asked why. She told him he was too young. She said Peter was wicked. That's why I don't want to think about Charlie anymore, or boys. I didn't sin, but I could have.

Thursday, June 11, 1959 *K.I.R.S.*

I PUNCHED Edna today. I knew she was going to come after me because I told her to shut up last week. All week she's been glaring at me and showing me her fist. It happened today just before lunch when Sister was out. Edna grabbed me from behind. This time I felt it coming and I twisted out of her reach and stood up.

"So you think you're tough, eh, shamah?"

"Why don't you leave me alone?" I said.

"I suppose you'll tell your sister Dorothy if we have a fight," she said.

"No," I said. "I won't."

"Let's go then," she said, slapping the top of my head.

When we got to the lavatory I stood in front of her with my fists curled by my sides, breathing hard.

She lifted her arm to hit my head and I slammed my fist into her tummy. I was surprised when she doubled over. I stepped back. She looked up with big tears rolling down her cheeks. Then she turned around and walked out. Pretty soon she came back in with her two grade eight friends.

One of them called Trina said, "What's going on around here? Why are you picking on Edna?"

I curled up my fists again and said, "She's the one who calls me shamah. I'm not. I'm a halfbreed. Besides she was making fun of Charlie. Charlie's dead."

"Oh," they said, looking at each other. They told Edna she shouldn't make fun of the dead.

Edna said she wasn't. Nobody said anything for awhile. Then Trina said they should go listen to the radio in the rec. They told me to leave Edna alone, and they left.

I thought they were going to gang up on me later, but they didn't. They kept whispering to each other and looking at me, but they left me alone. After school, Edna said hi to me. I didn't know what to do, so I said hi back to her, but I didn't smile. Neither of us did.

Saturday, June 20, 1959   Joyaska Ranch

I CAN'T believe we're home. This morning we
climbed on the bus with our suitcases and headed for
Firefly. We all sat together, Cookie and me, Missy
with Dorothy and Pearl with Rowdy. We all seemed
to lean forward, looking ahead for the first sign of
home. First it was Bird Lake where my dad used to
visit an old trapper called Johnny Cabou. Then it
was the logging camp where Aunt Mamie used to
live. Then that place at the end of the lake where we
saw a thousand trumpeter swans one time.

When we got to Quiltcana, some of the parents
were waiting by the side of the road with big smiles,
waving branches because the mosquitoes were so
thick. They hugged their children, and we felt jealous
that they were home first. They were so happy they
didn't even stop to wave goodbye to us.

The next place was the little town of Trading Post
where Uncle Tommy and Aunt Ella stay sometimes.
From there we could see Cody Mountain and then
we got really excited because we could see where
home is, at the bottom of the mountain, right in the
middle. When we passed the place where two big
irrigation pipes come to the highway, we let out a
yell all together. "Yahoo, we made it!"

Then I saw Mum at the bus station holding Benny's hand. I felt like crying, but I knew I couldn't so
I laughed. It sounded like someone was choking me.

Mum hugged me hard and kissed the top of my head. My dad shook my hand, then Dorothy's and Missy's. Then Benny lifted his T-shirt and showed us where lightning struck him on the tummy. It looked like a white scratch.

My dad drove over to the New York Restaurant and bought us all ice cream cones. That's always our big treat. Then we went home. We looked at the fields, the trees and the corrals with the horses in them to see if anything had changed. Then there in the middle of the hayfield was our house with the porch, the lilac bushes, the bay window with its flowered curtains. Then Spud was running out to meet us barking and barking, leaping up to lick our faces.

Mum cooked us deer steaks and fried potatoes and macaroni and carrots and homemade bread and, of course, apple pie, all our favourites. She told us to run out and play. The first place we went was the wild strawberry patch up at the flume where the prickly pears grow. Then to the barn to visit the horses, and all around the ranch.

I am here now in the apple tree, my favourite tree in the whole world. I can see Dad up at the barn with Missy and Benny. Dorothy and Jimmy are in the porch arguing. Mum's throwing scraps out to the chickens calling, "Here, chick, chick, chick." It's getting dark and the stars are coming out. Maybe I'll cry now.

TODAY my dad and I ploughed the potato field. He waits every summer for me to come home to help him. Everybody else plants potatoes in May. What we do is put the harness on Daisy, my mum's horse. She's part Clydesdale, very strong and gentle. Then Dad hooks up the plough to the harness. After that I ride Daisy to guide her to make straight rows and to keep her from going too fast. Dad holds the plough. It's pretty hard to sit on Daisy all day and to make sure she walks in a straight line. She has a sharp backbone.

My dad cusses a lot when we're ploughing. Mum said he must have got into the habit in the army. He was a sharpshooter and got wounded in the chest and foot at Vimy Ridge in France. He never talks about the war unless he's drinking. Then he yells and throws dishes around or anything he can get his hands on. Sometimes he keeps it up all night. Then he cries. He said once that the Germans they killed were just boys.

When Dad gets like that we usually grab our coats and run into the hills with Mum. We sleep under a tree. When we go home in the morning, my dad is usually up and whistling and cooking something to eat. He asks us where we were. When Mum tells him how he was acting he doesn't believe her.

This year Dorothy got a summer job cleaning

house and cooking for this family in town. She left on Monday and she only gets to come home on weekends sometimes. I'm glad she's away. She gets really bossy when she's at home. She makes us take turns doing dishes. Jimmy gets mad at her too, and they fight sometimes. One time when he was teasing her too much she waited behind the kitchen door, then clobbered him with a frying pan. After that she hid all afternoon. Then she found out from Mum that Jimmy went to town right after she hit him. Other times they are good friends. They play cards and talk.

Jimmy got a summer job too, as a ranch hand. He works until late at night. In September he will go away to university. He won a scholarship when he graduated. I had to ask Dorothy how to spell all these words. She asked me why I wanted to know. I told her I was going to write a letter to a school friend.

I never let Dorothy or Jimmy see my journal. They would make fun of me. One time I wrote a story about our dog Spud, and Jimmy read it and laughed and laughed.

Missy and Benny and I are the only ones home with Mum and Dad now. Our chores are feeding the chickens and pigs, packing wood, weeding the garden and sweeping floors. The cows are up in the range during summer so the grass can grow tall enough to cut for hay. After Dad cuts the grass the first week of July, we will have to help with the haying. Benny's the water boy. He brings Freshie around to the workers. When the hay's dry we use pitchforks to make little stacks, then load them onto the sloop. I like haying because we get to ride the horses down to the pond to water them, or down to the river after haying to go swimming and fishing.

When my parents go hunting we tell each other stories. We talk about our dreams or movies that we've seen. That way Missy and Benny don't get scared of us being alone. But when Mum's home I like to scare them. One time I showed them the heat rash on my arm and told them it was leprosy. I told them it would spread to them and make their flesh rot off their bodies. When they ran away from me I chased them and they screamed. They paid me back by locking me in the outhouse. I had to fold up a page of the Sears catalogue and push it through the crack to open the door.

Sometimes Cookie and Rowdy and Pearl visit us, and we read comics or play Hide and Go Seek around the little haystacks out on the field. Other times we walk to the river to go swimming. When we were small, Cookie and I made mudpies and Rowdy ate them. Rowdy's kind of chubby and he eats anything.

On Saturdays Dad drives us downtown to the matinee to watch a movie. It costs twenty cents each for kids under fourteen. Pop, popcorn, chocolate bars or a bag of candy costs 10 cents.

My favourite movie is *My Friend Flicka*. I read the book about four times. Flicka was a horse, a mare, and she was the best friend of this boy. I wish I could have my own horse too, but I'm away at school most of the time.

Thursday, July 2, 1959 Joyaska Ranch

THE nuns at school punish us when we make a mistake, but never say a word about the good things we do. Mrs. Quill is like that. She is an old Indian woman with pale skin who lives in an unpainted house at the edge of our ranch just where the road meets the highway. She's my dad's aunt and I think she hates us.

Mum and Dad are good to her too. Dad always gives her meat when he goes hunting. After Mum milks Bossy every morning she scalds the milk. Then she puts some in a pail and tells one of us to take it to Mrs. Quill. Dorothy used to do it. Now it's me, and Benny and Missy go along for the walk. We tell stories or sing as we go. When we give the milk to Mrs. Quill she just tells us to put it on the table. She never says thank you or invites us in.

Mrs. Quill is skinny. She has white hair with a red kerchief tied around it, mean little eyes and a screechy voice. Sometimes when we're playing around that part of the ranch she screeches at us to pick her some choke-cherries. We don't mind. It's easy and you can fill a bucket fast. What we don't like is the way she stares at us squinty-eyed, then rolls her eye back until it's white. It's scary. When we told my mum about the choke-cherries she laughed. She said Mrs. Quill likes her home brew.

Last week Mrs. Quill stole Missy and hid her. My mum walked over with Benny and Missy that day to take her some milk. When Mum walked across the road to take milk to Cookie's mum, she noticed Missy was missing. So she went back and asked Mrs. Quill if Missy was there. Mrs. Quill said no. Mum got scared and looked all over the ranch for Missy. She was going to run downtown and get the police when Mrs. Quill told her she had Missy in her house. Mrs. Quill was laughing like it was a big joke.

After that Missy got really thin, and all her mosquito bites turned to sores. She kept crying and scratching. She wouldn't eat. My dad told Mum to make her a little picnic every day. Then he went out and bought her six white ducks. We call them Missy's ducks. They sleep in the chicken house and swim in the pond beside the well. Our favourite one is Chun Chully. He trips over his feet all the time and when he quacks he says "Quay-quay-quay" really loud. He makes us laugh. Sometimes Missy follows her ducks and plays beside them all day. She feeds them wheat and leftovers.

Thursday, July 9, 1959 Joyaska Ranch

I AM sitting in the apple tree looking at Joyaska Ranch. Dad says it's over a hundred acres, mostly fields of alfalfa, clover and timothy grass to feed our cattle and horses. The house is built of cedar planks with cedar shakes on the roof which are almost black because they are so old. The house has bay windows, a porch in front, and a verandah at back. Mum's lilac bushes and two tall trees stand in front of the porch. Behind the house there is a woodshed, meathouse, the vegetable garden, the well and the pond. Farther off is the chicken house and the outhouse, and the trail that leads to the river. Right below me is my dad's truck, a 1948 Fargo pick-up, navy blue.

Sometimes when my dad goes to town he lets us kids ride in the back of the truck so we can open the gate for him. Then we walk home. When I open the gate I like standing on the lowest pole and riding it as it swings open by itself.

Missy likes to picnic there outside the gate under the trembling aspen where an old log has fallen across the road. Every day she takes her little lunch up the road to her spot.

Past the three tall cottonwoods to the left the road goes straight through pine trees where an old grey log fence zigzags along the road. That's where Jimmy planted some strawberries. It's a nice place to sit in the cool grass and tell stories on a hot day.

After you pass Jimmy's secret strawberry place, the creek crosses the road. If you follow the creek into the trees you come to the place where dad puts the stillborn calves. Coyotes come there at night to eat the carcasses. When they howl it sounds spooky like ghosts. Our dog Spud barks at them.

At the dead calf tree you can see round circles in the ground, where Mum says the old Indians used to build their winter houses partly underground. They dug big round holes in the ground, then built log roofs over them. They stayed there in the winter when there was snow on the ground. The Indian word for it is shee-eesht-kin, meaning underground house.

Thursday, July 16, 1959 Joyaska Ranch

TODAY I heard some of my boy cousins talking about me. I was sitting in the apple tree when Sonny, Mickey and Rowdy walked by on their way to visit Jimmy and play his guitar because Jimmy came home early today. My cousins didn't see me. They said I was the only plain Stone girl. I know what plain means. It means the opposite of pretty. I couldn't believe my ears. I always thought I was beautiful because I have hazel-green eyes. Besides, Cookie told me that I look like Doris Day, my favourite actress.

I went running into my mum's bedroom where there is a big mirror on the dresser. I stared at myself for a long time. My hair is ugly because I have the junior girl "bowl" haircut, but all the other girls have it too. I looked at my eyes, sleepy looking and grey-green with yellow near the irises. Ski-jump nose. Medium lips. Dimple on my chin. Big ears but they don't stick out or show very much. Freckles.

I thought of Shirley Temple with her big blue eyes and curly hair. Then I knew it was true. I am plain. It makes you really sad to find out something like that.

I went around in a daze for the whole day wondering what I could do about it. Then I got the brush, the comb, some lipstick and rouge that was left here by Aunt Mamie, Cookie's mum. I combed and brushed my hair and pinned it behind my ears with bobby pins. I put on lipstick and rouge. I didn't look any better. I was putting eyebrow pencil on when Benny and Missy saw me. They watched for awhile. Then they climbed up on the basin stand with me and started trying on lipstick. They started arguing about which of them was the best-looking. Missy asked me what I thought. I looked at them. They both looked back at me, waiting.

"Well," I said. "Missy's the prettiest, and Benny's the cutest." They both looked happy when I said that.

After that I went to my mum and asked her if she thought I was plain. She said it was too soon to tell. You look like your dad, she told me. I went and looked at myself again. I couldn't see it, except for the eyes. Mum says Dad has wolf eyes, yellow eyes. I liked that but I was still sad.

One time Dorothy pushed my head back and asked if she could look at my nostrils. "You have the most beautiful nostrils," she said. Nostrils are nose holes. She said Jane Russell has beautiful nostrils too. Jane Russell is Dorothy's favourite movie star. She must have seen Jane Russell kissing with her head way back in a movie or a movie magazine. It doesn't help to have beautiful nostrils. Nobody can see them.

Then my dad came home, and he was a little tipsy.

"McSpoot," he said, "you're a square-shooter, and you have a million-dollar smile." A square-shooter is an honest person. I went and smiled at myself in the mirror. It pushed up the corners of my eyes and looked so merry. "It's true," I said. "I have a million-dollar smile."

Thursday, July 23, 1959 Joyaska Ranch

ONE of Missy's ducks hatched three little ducklings. The mother duck brought them right down to the pond near the well and they all went in. They were so small and yellow paddling around on the water. We couldn't believe they could swim when they're only one day old.

Two of the chickens hatched eggs too, so we have thirteen new chicks. When we go too near the chicks the mother hen gets worried and spreads her wings out and covers them.

My dad did a funny thing though. He put two duck eggs under one of the hens, and she hatched two ducklings along with six chicks. The hen treats the ducklings like her own chicks. The only thing is when they went near the pond the ducklings went in for a swim. The poor mother hen almost went crazy. She went running around the pond to the left, then to the right. She almost ran into the pond. She was clucking at them, trying to call them. Finally they came out and the hen felt better. She led them away from the water.

Ducklings and chicks are different in another way too. Ducklings always walk in a single file. Chicks walk all over the place. Chicks scratch in the ground like chickens, but ducks don't. Also duck eggs are bigger.

Missy seems to be getting better now that she has the ducks to look after. Her sores are healing and she's eating more. My dad said she was the only one who could feed the ducks. She has to make sure they're in the chicken house at night. Otherwise an owl or hawk or weasel could kill and eat them.

Now Missy's getting better, but Dorothy had a nightmare when she came home last weekend. In her dream she was being chased across the field by a big mean bull. There was no place for her to hide. That's when she woke up screaming. She jumped up and ran in the dark across the bed, fell onto the floor, got up and tried to run through the wall. My dad got a flashlight and came to see what the matter was. Then Dorothy woke up with a sprained ankle. She was crying and Mum talked to her and held her for awhile. She told Mum that same nightmare started at school and keeps coming back. Sometimes she wakes up standing beside her bed. Once she woke up in the broom closet.

I never had a nightmare, but a strange thing happened one time at school. I woke up really cold because I had no blankets on. They were gone. I looked all over for them and couldn't find them. Finally I had to knock on Sister's door and tell her because it was so cold that our breaths were clouding even though we were inside. Sister helped me look for my blankets and we still couldn't find them. She went and got me some blankets from the Sisters' closet. Later one of the girls found my blankets under the rubber stand downstairs in the rec. I don't know how they got there, but it scared me.

Thursday, July 30, 1959   Joyaska Ranch

TODAY we held a funeral for Bambi, our fawn. There was Missy and Cookie and Rowdy and Benny and me. We dug a hole near the fence, found a cardboard box to put Bambi in, and covered it over again. We said a prayer and put a cross on the grave. We said goodbye to Bambi, and we cried.

My dad brought the fawn home about a week ago because he found the mother dead up in the hills where he was checking for cattle. Somebody shot her. Dad says never shoot deer in summer because that's when the females have their babies.

Mum gave the fawn some cow milk in a baby bottle every day after she milked Bossy. She thinks the cow milk was too rich for it, that's why it died. My dad says it must have got scared and died of shock. He asked us if we scared it or chased it around, but we didn't. We think our cousin Mickey shot it with his sling shot. He does that to birds. Dad caught him once and told him never to kill animals unless you need to eat. Dad said never to make animals suffer.

We used to have a baby bear too, when I was eight. Her name was Pa-cheet, which means baby bear. Somebody shot the mother bear, and they found the baby and brought it to my dad. Dorothy used to play with Pa-cheet. She would kneel down and call Pa-cheet to jump on her back. Then she'd grab Pa-cheet's front paws and flip her over her head. Pa-cheet would go rolling over and over, then get up on Dorothy's back for more. Pa-cheet used to get lonely and cry at night.

When she got bigger Pa-cheet used to scare us when she got too rough. She started to get into the food all the time. She dug in Mum's cupboards and spilled flour and sugar all over the kitchen. Once she chased Missy and me up onto Mum's bed because she smelled the boxes of plums and pears under the bed. She started growling and clawing at us. She wanted all the fruit to herself. Mum got mad and told my dad to do something about it. He chained her up to the dog-house, but soon she got big enough to break the chain. That's when my dad drove her up into the mountain and dropped her off. Next day she was back on the porch crying for food. I think my dad gave her to the wildlife people after that.

We've buried other animals down by the fence. There's a duckling, a bird with a broken wing, our cat Otter, Chipper our old collie, and there was Henrietta the chick who was born with one leg backwards. She was my special pet. I used to feed her and every night I put her in one of my dad's wool socks that I hung on a nail on the wall. You could hear her cheeping softly just like chicks do when they are under the mother hen's wings. She died when Jimmy sat on her. He was sorry about it. He didn't see her because she was in her sock. I was mad at Jimmy for awhile after that.

I thought about Charlie today too when we prayed for Bambi. He had no dad, only a mum. He was probably trying to fish for her when he drowned. I got mad at Charlie and felt like cussing. I thought about him fishing at the edge of the river and falling in on purpose. Then I knew it couldn't be. He'd have been wearing a white T-shirt and old khaki pants, probably an old hat. I don't know if he was fishing with a pole or helping somebody net fish. Maybe he was just walking by and tripped.

Once I saw a bigger boy picking on Charlie, shoving him. Calling him names. Skinny as he was, Charlie pushed back, ready to fight.

Charlie wouldn't have gone in on purpose. He wouldn't have given up. He wouldn't have been drinking alcohol and fallen in accidently. He just fell into the river and didn't make it out.

I thought about the old T-shirt he always wore, kind of big on him and always clean. I thought of what he might say if he could be here for a minute. Then tears came in big drops down my face.

LAST night I talked to my dad about God. He came home drunk and he was hollering around like usual, so I got mad at him. I told him not to drink. I told him to pray. He looked at me for a long time. Then he sat down and listened to me with his face in his hands. At first I thought he was laughing. Then I thought maybe he was crying.

After that I didn't know what to do so I jumped up on the chair and got the holy picture down from the little shelf in the living room. It was a picture of Jesus dying on the cross. There, I told Dad, look at Jesus. He died on the cross for you, for all of us. Pray, and stop your drinking. Stop cussing. Stop fighting with Mum. Dad, bad people go to hell. After that he got up and stumbled into the other room and closed the door.

I don't know if I did the right thing or not. But he embarrassed us when the missionary came for Sunday dinner after Mass. Mum cooked all morning while Dorothy, Missy and me went with Father Jeremy to the Sunday service at the Ntslatko Reserve. Mum cooked chicken and gravy and mashed potatoes and carrots and homemade rootbeer and fresh buns and plum pudding. Then Dad had to bring Uncle Willy home.

Uncle hates priests since the time one tried to do something wicked to him. And sure enough Uncle had a mickey. He and dad were talking loud and singing by the time the priest came. What are we going to do, we asked Mum.

We went to the bedroom where they were singing loud and sharing a bottle. "Quick, lock them in," said Dorothy. I grabbed the inside doorknob, unscrewed it, pulled it out and we slammed the door shut. They didn't even notice. They kept right on with their party.

When Father Jeremy came he had a nice dinner and chatted with my mum and sisters. Every once in a while we could hear a shout from the room, or a loud laugh, but we all pretended not to hear. Father Jeremy looked at me and winked when we heard a loud cuss.

Then Uncle started banging on the door. "Let me out," he hollered. "I need to take a leak." I ran over and told him the door broke and we were looking for the doorknob. It kept him quiet for about one minute. Then Father Jeremy said it was time to go, and he was thanking Mum for dinner. As we all walked past the door we could see the end of a pair of scissors poking through the doorknob hole, going chook, chook, chook. They got it open just as Father Jeremy climbed into his car. Uncle Willy made a beeline for the outhouse. My dad came out and watched Father Jeremy drive away. "Jesus was poor," he said. "They drive fancy new cars."

Dorothy got mad and asked what were they supposed to do. Walk?

Later we were wondering about Dad's chances of making it to heaven. Dorothy says everybody sins. The thing is to get to confession for a blessing from a priest. But once when I walked by the barn I heard Dad crying and saying sorry to God when he didn't know anyone was around.

Thursday, August 13, 1959 Joyaska Ranch

WHEN I was sweeping the floor in Father Sloane's room last year I found a little keychain with a music box in it. It was gold coloured with a little wind-up handle like a watch at the back. I asked Father what it was. He wound it up for me and told me I could play it anytime I wanted to. I put it close to my ear. The music sounded like a tiny harp. Father said it was classical music, but he couldn't quite remember the name of it.

Every day I used to hurry with the clean-up so I could play the music box. I felt it belonged to me somehow. Like it was telling my story or playing my song. When June came and it was time to go home, Father told me I could have it. I was so happy I kept it in my pocket all the time.

At home I let Benny and Missy listen to it. They

liked the music too. We played it over and over and made up stories about it. Maybe the composer made up the tune in honour of a beautiful girl who died, or a boy saw angels who told him to share the tune to heal people all over the world.

Yesterday my mum and dad took us to Moon Ranch where Yay-yah lives. It's the same place where we look for river mushrooms in the spring under the cottonwood leaves. The big people started to talk in Indian. We couldn't understand what they were saying so we went outside to play.

As usual we brought the music box. We were close to the woods and we thought up good stories about the little people that Yay-yah says live in holes in the ground. She hears them laughing sometimes when she waters the horses in the evening, just before it gets really dark. She even saw one late one evening, way up in the mountains where she was picking berries. She said it was about three feet tall and really ugly. We thought they would love to get their hands on the music box and listen to that wonderful tune. It would be just the right size for them. We wound it up and put it on an old tree stump so they could hear it.

Not long after that Mum called us into the cabin to have tea. I thought Benny or Missy had the music box, and they thought I had it, but none of us did. When we went out to look for it, it was gone. We looked all over, but we couldn't find it. Pretty soon my dad said we had to go and we climbed into the back of the truck and drove away. In one way I felt sad to lose my music box, and in another I felt happy because maybe the little people really did like it. Benny asked Missy if she thought the little people took it. Missy asked me what I thought.

"Did either of you take it?" I asked.

"No," they said.

"Then it might have been the little people," I said. We smiled all the way home.

Thursday, August 20, 1959 Joyaska Ranch

MY Aunt Alice died. When somebody dies at home we have a big gathering, called a potlatch. Lots of people come from all over and stay for about a week. If they are from out of town they camp with relatives on the reserve. We only went for the day because Dad's busy haying right now.

Mum said we're not supposed to laugh or talk loud, or run around and make noise when somebody dies. She told me and Missy to wear the dresses she made us out of cotton flour sacks. My dad brought some deer meat to feed the people, and Mum brought some canned huckleberries.

My Aunt Alice's body was in the house. Mum told us not to go in there, but we could hear the people praying and singing from outside. Sometimes they sing hymns in Indian. I know when they are making the sign of the cross, because they put their right hands on their foreheads, chests, left shoulders and right shoulders. We make the sign of the cross too, at school. It wards off devils, Sister Theo says.

My dad started talking and visiting with some other men, and Mum went in to help in the kitchen. Us kids went around the back of the house to watch the men carving out Aunt Alice's name on the wood headstone. The wood shavings smelt nice like the pine sap that we eat in the early spring. We saw some kids there but we didn't know them because our ranch is at the opposite end of the valley.

After awhile the priest came and some men carried Aunt Alice's coffin to the church for Mass. The people followed singing hymns and praying and crying. We sat outside in the truck. My dad won't go inside a church. When he sees the priests he spits. He doesn't like priests. He says priests are not as holy as they like us to think.

When the bell started ringing everybody came out and we drove to the graveyard. I didn't see what happened. After that everyone went back to Aunt Alice's house and ate dinner. We ate fried deer steaks with gravy or deer meat roasted and sliced. There was salmon, potatoes, rice and carrots. An old man Mum said was the chief said grace. He asked God to bless the food.

After that we all ate. Suddenly Missy spoke up

and said in a loud voice, "Salt, please." The chief looked at her sitting there so tiny. He said some Indian words and everybody laughed and somebody passed her the salt. The chief said Missy is small but she has a big voice.

After awhile somebody started a bonfire and people lined up to play lahal, the stick game. That's when my dad said we were going home. As we drove away we could see people around the fire still laughing and placing bets.

Thursday, August 27, 1959 Joyaska Ranch

TODAY my dad saddled up the horses and took me and Benny and Missy up the mountain to Cody Canyon. He wanted to clear the creek that flows down from the beaver pond into our hayfields. Dad wants to get one more hay crop this fall.

Mum packed us a lunch of bannock, canned salmon, apples, and a Thermos of tea. Dad put the lunch in his saddle bag and tied his shovel to the rifle scabbard behind the saddle.

Dad told me to ride behind the saddle on Baldy with him. Benny and Missy rode Daisy, Mum's old saddle horse. Maybe Dad wanted to see how Missy would handle Daisy on her own.

We rode behind the barn and straight up the side of the mountain on a steep deer trail through the trees. All we could hear were the horses' hooves clicking against rocks, the saddles squeaking and a crow cawing at the top of an old dead pine tree. My dad grinned at the crow and said, "Don't scare the deer."

When we got to the top of the trail we saw thousands of purply-pink flowers all together in the tall grass along the creek. We stopped and looked at it for awhile because it was so pretty. "Fireweed," said Dad.

We rode past a bare hillside with millions of wildflowers and yellow grass, and sagebrush in bloom. When we stopped my dad showed us where to pick raspberries around a big stump near a tiny bubbling brook. In the high mountains the berries get ripe late. Dad told us to eat our lunch if we got hungry. Then he tethered the horses, walked over to the beaver pond and started to shovel the creek where it was blocked by sticks and dirt and rocks.

Missy and I went around to the shady part of the bush to pick the raspberries. They were sweet and warm from the sun. Benny went over to the brook to scoop up water in a little tin cup. Then he sneaked over to Missy and spilled some down her back. She screeched and they both started to laugh and splash each other with water. While they were playing I climbed up on Baldy and pretended to be a trick rider standing on the saddle, then hanging low on one side.

I went back to the brook and we sat watching Dad work. We talked about going back to school, about how much we hate it there. We felt sad because we have to go back next week.

When the shadows were getting long Dad came over and got a drink with Benny's little cup. Then he took off his cowboy hat and wiped his forehead, looking around at the valley below. He looked tired.

"It's going to get crowded in the valley in a few years," he said. "People will be building houses all around the ranch. Ranching won't pay much anymore. You kids want to get yourselves an education. Get a job. That way you'll be okay."

Missy and I looked at each other. How did he know we were talking about school?

By the time we got back it was almost dark and Mum had supper waiting. Dad said we're going up the mountain to pick huckleberries tomorrow. We'll pick berries in the afternoon, camp the night, pick berries again in the morning and come home on Saturday. Then we'll have to pack water so Mum can wash our clothes for school, and Dad will probably buy me and Missy new shoes and sweaters and socks. He'll buy Benny a shirt, jeans and shoes. He always buys us new clothes when we go back to school. It's our pay for helping put up the hay.

Benny and Missy are sleeping now and I can hear Mum and Dad talking and laughing in the kitchen. Jimmy is playing the guitar. Dorothy will be coming home from her job on Saturday. I'm writing my journal entry, the last one before I go back to school.

I think I'll leave the journal at home in the attic inside my dad's old violin case. If Yay-yah is in the mountains where we go to pick berries, I'll ask her to make a buckskin cover for it. I'll ask her to bead fireweed flowers on it.